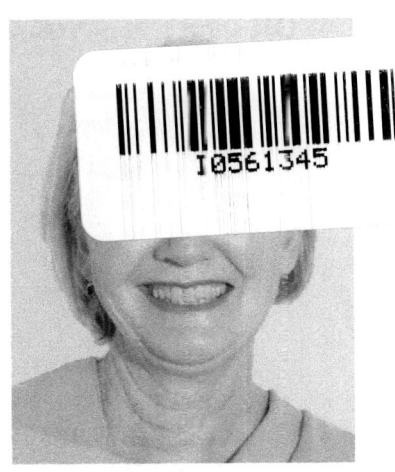

Karen grew up in a small country town in north-eastern Victoria, Australia. She spent her childhood riding horses through beautiful scenery of eucalypts, lakes, and snow-capped mountains and her love of landscape deeply affects her writing. She worked in a range of educational settings and holds a Ph.D. and M.Ed. (Hons) in the areas of fantasy. She is particularly interested in the power of the hero's inner journey which she explores through Deep Fantasy. Karen has travelled extensively overseas but enjoys nothing more than camping in the Australian Outback. She lives in Melbourne and now writes full-time. You can find out more about Karen and her books on her website.

Connect with K. S. Nikakis

Amazon: https://www.amazon.com/author/ksnikakis
Twitter: https://twitter.com/KSNikakis
Facebook: www.facebook.com/ksnikakis
Goodreads: www.goodreads.com
Website: www.ksnikakis.com
Email: author@ksnikakis.com

WORKS BY K S NIKAKIS

Non Fiction

Journey: Seeking the Sacred, Spirit and Soul in the Australian Wilderness

Fantasy Novels
Series

Angel Caste series:
Angel Blood
Angel Breath
Angel Bone
Angel Bound
Angel Blessed
Angel Caste – Complete 5 Book Series

The Kira Chronicles trilogy:*
The Whisper of Leaves
The Song of the Silvercades
The Cry of the Marwing
remnant hard copies only

The Kira Chronicles series:
The Whisper of Leaves
The Silence of Stone
The Secrets of Stars
The Thunder of Hoofs
The Crying of Birds
The Music of Home
The Kira Chronicles – Complete 6 Book Series

Fantasy Novels

The Emerald Serpent
Heart Hunter
The Third Moon
Messenger
I Heard the Wolf Call My Name – *Finalist - Best YA
Novel Aurealis Awards, 2019*

Fantasy Short Stories

The Gift
The Tale of Prince Anura
Dragon Sprite
Glass-Heart – *Finalist – Best YA
Short Story Aurealis Awards, 2019*

THE CRYING OF BIRDS

K.S. NIKAKIS

First published by SOV CONSULTING LLC - SOV
Media Australia 2018
Amazon: www.amazon.com.au

The Crying of Birds Book 5 The Kira Chronicles Series
© copyright by KS Nikakis 2018

Publisher: SOV CONSULTING LLC - SOV Media
Melbourne, Australia.

Cover by AS Nikakis: http://asnikakis.com
Shutterstock.com/nutriaaa

National Library of Australia
Cataloguing-in-Publication entry:
Nikakis, Karen Simpson
The Crying of Birds Book 5 The Kira Chronicles Series
ISBN 978-0-6489797-1-5

For Poppy and Terry Nikakis

THE CRYING OF BIRDS

MAP OF NORTHERN LANDS

The Tremen

Of the Bough – Tremen heart of healing
Maxen (dec) – Kashclan - Tremen Leader
Fasarini (dec) – Sarclan – bondmate of Maxen
Merek (dec) – eldest son of Maxen
Lern (dec) – second eldest son of Maxen
Kiraon (Kira) – Tremen Leader - daughter of Maxen
Kandor (dec) – youngest son of Maxen
Sendra (dec) (helper) – Sarclan

Kashclan – descended from Kasheron
Miken – Clanleader
Tenerini – Barclan – bondmate of Miken
Tresen – son of Miken
Mikini – daughter of Miken
Brem – experienced Healer and Protector
Arlen – learner Healer and Protector; Healer volunteer
Paterek – learner Healer and Protector
Werem – learner Healer and Protector
Kertash – Protector Leader

Sarclan – descended from Sarkash
Berendash – Clanleader

Tarclan – descended from Taren
Farish – (dec) Clanleader
Kemrick - Clanleader
Sarkash – (dec) Protector Commander

Morclan – descended from Mormesh
Marren – Clanleader
Kest – Protector Commander
Kesilini – sister of Kest
Feseren – (dec) Protector
Misilini – Barclan – bondmate of Feseren
Penedrin – Protector

Renclan – descended from Renen
Sanden – Clanleader
Pekrash – Protector Leader, Commander of Tremen
volunteers
Sanaken – (dec) Protector

Kenclan – descended from Kentash
Tenedren – Clanleader
Senden – Protector Leader

Barclan – descended from Baren
Ketten – Clanleader

Sherclan – descended from Sheren
Dakresh – Clanleader
Sener – elder son of Dakresh
Bern – (dec) younger son of Dakresh
Bendrash – Protector Leader

Tallien
Caledon e Saridon e Talliel – Placidien
Roshai – sister of Caledon
Pisa – youngest daughter of Roshai
Mechtlin – husband of Roshai

Tain
Beris – King
Adris – Prince, son of Beris
King's Guard
Remas – Guard Leader
Ather – Second Leader
Belzen
Archorn

Troopsmen
Dorchen – Commander
Selvet – Troop Leader
Somer
Tardich
Derz

Physicks
Dumer – Physick General
Aranz – Major Physick
Speri – lesser physick

Gatherer
Jaitich

Terak Kirillian
Rulership
Tierken – Feailner
Laryia – sister of Tierken
Darid (dec) – last Feailner, uncle of Tierken
Merench (dec) father to Tierken and Laryia
Lyess (dec) mother to Tierken and Laryia
Poerin – military trainer of Tierken

Marken
Rosham – father of Farid
Milsin
Borsten
Gelf

Domain
Farid – Keeper of the Domain
Ryn – Horse Master
Mouras – Room Master
Niria – server, wife to Marin

Domain Guard
Tharin – Guard Leader
Daril – Guard Second
Storsil
Farsrin

Patrolmen
Marin – Patrol Commander
Jonred – Patrol Leader
Slivkash
Anvorn
Nordrin
Arnil
Barid
Ralin
Sarim
Serden
Derkash
Ayled
Shird
Vardrin

Jarvid
Wirinkash
Farian
Kanil

Kessomi
Eris – Darid and Merench's mother; grandmother to Tierken and Laryia
Thalli – childhood friend of Laryia
Leos – husband of Thalli
Jafiel – brother of Leos
Kira – baby daughter of Thalli
Robrin – stable master

The Shargh
Cashgar

Erboran – (dec) Chief
Arkendrin – younger brother of Erboran
Ergardrin (dec) – father of Erboran and Arkendrin
Tarkenda – join-wife of Ergardrin - mother of Erboran and Arkendrin
Palansa – join-wife of Erboran – Chief-wife and Chief-mother – guardian of next Chief
Ersalan – baby son of Erboran and Palansa – next Chief
Sansula – friend to Palansa
Orsron – baby son of Sansula

Loyal to Erboran
Erdosin
Irsulalin
Ormadon
Erlken – Ormadon's son

Aronin – Ormadon's kin
Irslin – Ormadon's kin
Irmakin
and their blood-ties

Loyal to Arkendrin
Irason
Ermashin
Urpalin
Orthaken
Irdodun
Orlun
Urgundin (dec)
and their blood-ties

Weshargh
Orbdargan – Chief
Orfedren
Urugen

Soushargh
Yrshin – Chief

Ashmiri
Uthlin - Chief

Founders of the Four Shargh Peoples
The Cashgar Shargh – Artmenton
The Soushargh – Urchelen
The Weshargh – Irkardin
The Ashmiri - Ashmiridin

The Crying of Birds

Thus spoke the Last of the Shargh Tellers:

If Healer sees a setting sun
and gold meets gold, two halves are one,
then Westerner with silver tongue
will love and lose the golden one,
but bind a friendship slow begun.
If horses graze in forests deep
where trees their summer greening keep
then fire will be the flatswords' bane
and bring the dead to life again.
Deeds long past will hunt the Shargh
and funeral smoke consume the stars
until the thing that draws no breath,
devours the dark that feeds on death.

1

The stable door slammed in the wind and Kira jumped, still on edge from the journey north. The half patrol Marin led had suffered no attacks and the weather had been fair, unlike their miserable journey south and she wondered if her tension stemmed from leaving Tierken behind without farewell *or* from the sense of having been watched the entire journey.

The plain had seemed empty but the men had ridden with their bows unclipped for days. Marin had been unusually gruff too but she guessed that flowed from taking her North without the Feailner's *express* permission. Kira grimaced. Marin knew the terms of her trade with the Feailner as well as she did: three days in Maraschin to speak with the Protectors volunteers, in exchange for her returning to Sarnia and staying there.

Her cracked ribs had made the journey a nightmare but Sarnia must have a Haelen if its men were not to die. Even so, she had to be carried to her rooms and had dosed herself with sickleseed *and* slept for three days. Niria had been by her bed whenever she had roused and, in the end, she had only crawled from the covers because of the need to establish a Haelen.

The stable was in good repair but, according to Laryia, the stable had not been used in the time she and Tierken had been in Sarnia. It certainly smelled like it! Kira tried to wrest a shutter open to get fresh air but the hinges were stiff. 'Don't,' ordered Laryia. 'You're just from your bed.'

Kira sagged against a stall and one of the Domain Guard put his shoulder to the shutter and there was a harsh screech as it gave way. Laryia's concerned gaze was on her and Kira made an effort to straighten. 'It's the right layout for a Haelen,' she said. 'The stalls could be divided with curtains and the harness store made into a Herbery.'

There was water too, provided for the horses, and its location under the wall made it easy for carriers to access. Kira felt more cheerful but wondered if a message cylinder prohibiting the Haelen already made its way north. There had been a flow of messages from Maraschin and a flow of men, weapons, and supplies south.

She knew that word of her safe arrival had been sent to Maraschin and that there had already been fighting, which made the Haelen even more urgent. The thought of wounds, even those suffered by the Shargh, filled her dread.

They came back out into the cool morning air and started up the Domain path, the Guard at their heels. 'I'll organize for the stables to be cleared and scrubbed over the next few days,' said Laryia, taking Kira's arm to steady her. 'And I'll trade for some woodwrights.'

'I'll need to gather too,' said Kira. 'Are there herbs near the walls?'

Laryia shook her head. 'The land is pretty well-grazed.' She glanced at Kira sideways. 'Tierken's orders are that you remain *within* Sarnia. He's asked me to do the same.'

'He *orders* me but *asks* you?'

'He just wants us safe, that's all.'

'According to him, the fighting won't come north, so there's no risk,' said Kira tartly.

Laryia's lips compressed but she held her silence until they reached the Domain and the Guard peeled off to their station. 'I don't understand why Tierken's wish to protect you angers you so, Kira,' she said in a low voice as they made their way across the square. 'Don't Tremen men keep those they love safe?'

'I'm just worried about having enough herbs to heal,' muttered Kira, regretting having upset Laryia, but Laryia still looked annoyed when she left Kira at her rooms. Kira collapsed onto her bed and when the pain ebbed, hauled herself up and emptied her pack onto the cover. She had one pot of fireweed Tresen had given her in Maraschin and half a pot she had brought from Allogrenia, but the rest of her supplies were barely enough to fill a beginner-Healer's kit.

Steps sounded in the room outside and then Laryia appeared in the sleeping-room doorway. 'I've been thinking, Kira. We could get herbs from Kessom, but we would need to do so soon. Once snowmelt starts, Glass Gorge floods and the journey's too dangerous.'

'We would need a steady supply and some herbs are only potent when they're newly harvested,' said Kira doubtfully. 'I don't think fireweed grows there either, at least, I couldn't find any.'

Laryia came and perched on the bed. 'Is that what you were doing on our last day there?' she asked suddenly. 'Searching for fireweed?' Kira nodded. 'Tierken was frantic despite the Guard. Merench drowned on a night like that. I don't remember our father or our mother Lyess, but Tierken does. We think Merench was caught by floodwaters as he gathered in one of the small valleys below Kessom. They're narrow and fill quickly. His body was found in Glass Gorge.'

Kira recalled Tierken's reaction to her return and the argument that had followed but neither resolved her need for herbs. 'Is there nowhere in Sarnia that isn't stone?' she asked in frustration.

Laryia shrugged. 'The Wastes in the Caru Quarter.'

Kira's heart quickened. Of course! It was where she had fled after the Mid-market banquet and yet another argument with Tierken. There were alehouses there, and women who traded themselves, *and* a great hollow of land, rampant with weeds.

'Its correct name is Kasheron's Quarter,' added Laryia.

Kira stared at her in shock. '*Kasheron's* Quarter?'

'When Kasheron and his followers deser—*left*, Queen Kiraon insisted her other son, Terak, put aside a quarter of the city for them in case they returned. She even built a garden in the old quarry in case Kasheron came back. She found pleasure in it too, of course, being from Kessom.'

Laryia gave Kira's hand a squeeze. 'Ever since Tierken's been Feailner, Rosham's been at him to open it up to the other Quarters. The city's crowded and extending the wall is costly. I thought Tierken was going to agree last Feailmark and so did Rosham, but Tierken seems to have changed his mind. Rosham was *very* annoyed.'

'Are you saying Tierken believes Kasheron's people *will* return?' asked Kira, her heart skittering.

'I don't know what Tierken believes,' said Laryia, avoiding her eyes. 'Rosham's never been well-disposed towards Tierken, and sometimes Tierken loses patience and goads him.' She gave a small smile. 'Probably not the best idea given Rosham's influence.'

'Tierken's Feailner,' said Kira irritably. 'Why can't he do what he wants?'

'He can, but things run more smoothly with the Marken and trader's cooperation. Darid was Tierken's *uncle* not his father and gold eyes still carry the taint of Kasheron's leaving. Tierken had to carve out a place for himself in Sarnia. It wasn't just handed to him.'

12

'Then me being here undermines everything he's fought to achieve,' said Kira slowly. 'Maybe I should leave.'

Laryia's hand tightened on hers. 'It's not that clear-cut, Kira. After the long seasons of Darid's childless rule, Sarnia wants certainty. Many in the city would prefer to see the Feailner married to the woman he loves, gold-eyed or not, than remain unmarried. Sarnia wants an heir.'

Kira withdrew her hand. The idea of being part of the Sarnia's plan for succession was almost as repellent as being despised by them.

'Don't let it concern you,' continued Laryia. 'They'd like to see me married for the same reason, preferably to Farid, and carrying too. If the Feailner won't produce an heir then his sister should,' she added mockingly. 'But I'll choose who I marry and when.

'Of course, the city can't see why I haven't made the Marriage Walk with Farid already and in some ways, I can't either.' Kira stared at her in bewilderment. 'Don't you think he's handsome?' Kira nodded, remembering the stares of the women at the Mid-market banquet. 'And charming and pleasant?'

'He's kind and true,' said Kira.

'Yes,' agreed Laryia. 'Farid is a good friend but I don't love him, and there has to be love, doesn't there?'

'Yes, of course,' said Kira, but she already knew that, for a Feailner, things were rarely that simple.

Tierken watched the circling birds as he waited with his men around their fires. Adris said they were *marwings*, hunting birds from the southern Azurcades. Their harsh cries had been a backdrop to the fighting on the Baia Plain

13

but they were more like scavengers than hunters, drawn by the bodies of goats, horses and men.

Tierken's mouth twisted. Once he had wandered the Silvercades' deep valleys with Poerin, hunted wolves with Kir herders, galloped Kalos hard and fast over the Sarsalin just for the sheer joy of it, but now all he did was kill.

Nor was the slaughter all that troubled him. He had planned to take Kira North once her three days in Maraschin were up, if her injuries permitted it, but things had turned too fast especially after the Terak-Tain Alliance had been renewed, and he had become embroiled in the fighting.

He took several quick steps up and down as he considered her. She had complied with the terms of their trade with uncharacteristic self-discipline and gone North again on the third day *with cracked ribs and just half a patrol.* His breath hissed. He had no idea what possessed Marin to take her and the wait for confirmation she had reached Sarnia's safety had been agonizing.

Thank Irid, the news had been good and he could focus on building cooperation between his men and the Tremen. It had been quicker than he dared hope possible and he had not heard *Terak Kutan* muttered by the Tremen or *traitorous deserters* muttered by the Terak for over a moon quarter.

The patrolmen in Maraschin had witnessed Kira's kin-link claim and the news had spread quickly to those who had not, and had given rise to a curious state of affairs. The *Feailner* had ignored the claim and so they did too and the Protectors clearly wanted nothing to do with Kasheron's *barbaric* brother and yet, instead of creating ill-feeling, the Terak and Tremen had formed friendships. They shared a common tongue, which helped, but there seemed to be a genuine liking as well.

His hands came to his hips as he considered the growing evidence for Kira's kinship claim *if* the Tallien *Caledon e Saridon e Talliel* was to be believed. Virtually all the records the Tallien spoke of existed *outside* Sarnia, which was fortunate, as there were good reasons for Tierken not to acknowledge the link. Rosham would use it as a weapon against him and he could not fight effectively in the south if Farid's authority were undermined in the North. Kira was safely in Sarnia now anyway, and the Terak and Tremen fought together, so *if* he acknowledged any kin-link, it would be at the time and manner of *his* choosing.

Movement on the plain heralded the approach of Pekrash and the Tremen who, unlike the Terak, travelled on foot. Tierken had taken his men on ahead to strike camp and set traps but they roasted nuts as well as silverjacks, as some of the Tremen still refused to eat meat.

Adris and the Tallien hunted Shargh further east and sought to persuade Tain herders to take shelter in Maraschin. Adris had already moved his people from the ravaged settlements of Listlin Tor, Slift Tor and Mendor but the herders had yet to accept the bitter truth that The Westlans must be abandoned.

Tierken considered the Tain King as he waited. Adris burned what the Shargh had not already destroyed, a ruthless and heart-breaking strategy to deny them food and shelter when they were driven back. The weather on the Sarsalin did not soften until late spring and once The Westlans was secure, the Shargh would be hounded deep into its shelterless expanse.

15

Five to six days should be enough to exhaust the Shargh *if* they were kept on the run *and* away from Ashmiri succor. He and Adris would allow the Shargh to flee south but for the Shargh to regain the food and shelter of their own lands, they must breach the Terak-Tain-Tremen lines, fight their way through the King's Guard Adris had stationed at The Westlans, and cross the Azurcades. If things went to plan, Tierken should be back in Sarnia within the next moon.

The Tremen arrived in the formation Tierken had insisted on but which seemed alien to them, and he welcomed Pekrash to his fire and offered him a mug of cotzee. The Tremen preferred a concoction called thornyflower tea, and early in their time together, Pekrash had prepared a cup for Tierken. It tasted like stagnant water and Tierken was glad when Pekrash's supply had been used.

The Tremen Commander thanked Tierken but he held the metal cup with his fingertips as Kira did, and when Tierken tipped roasted nuts into a bowl, Pekrash thanked him again, once more reminding Tierken of Kira. *Kashclan thanks the Terak Feailner*, she would say, and then refuse to eat. He thought of the last time they had made love, her face suffused with tenderness for him, and closed his eyes.

'Your leg pains you, Terak Feailner?' asked Pekrash.

'Not really,' said Tierken. He had suffered a slash to his calf some days earlier and noticed that all the Protectors took a keen interest in easing the pain of others. *If* Kasheron *had* established the Tremen, he had instilled a powerful sense of nurturing and yet they could still fight, not with the Terak's strength, but with agility, speed and a surprising degree of discipline.

They were loyal to Pekrash as their Commander and it was clear they fought only to preserve Allogrenia but they were fascinated by everything they saw and listened wide-eyed to the patrolmen's tales of Terak's Tor, Sarnia, the Silvercades and the lands beyond the seas.

Tierken rose as Vardrin returned from scout but remained at the fire to receive the report. He needed to ensure Pekrash was privy to it, something he had failed to do early on. The Tallien had reminded him of the failure, with his usual respectful subtlety, and while the reprimand was unwelcome, it was deserved. *You command the Terak Kirillian, Feailner, Pekrash the Tremen, and King Adris the Tain, but we all fight together. If our left hand is weaker than our right, it strengthens both hands of the Shargh.*

Tierken had since made an effort to include the Tremen Commander in his thoughts, as well as reports, and what had begun as a careful politeness between them had become, if not friendship, then certainly respect and trust. Now Tierken saw that Pekrash was troubled. 'If the Shargh are on the plain, perhaps we should have sighted them,' he said.

'And as we haven't, they might have slid to our flanks or bypassed us and gone further north?'

'Perhaps, Terak Feailner.'

Tierken thought it unlikely, given the good visibility on this part of the Sarsalin, and the attacks near Maraschin, but he went to where his men ate, and ordered Shird and Nordrin out on scout.

Tresen was waiting with his Healer's kit when he returned. 'Time to dress that wound, Feailner,' he said.

Tierken obediently pulled off his boot and eased up his trousers to reveal his heavily bandaged calf. The wound had needed more than twenty stitches but the sword had been aimed at Kalos would have killed the stallion had Tierken not thrown his leg back. Thanks to Tresen's quick attention and a liberal dose of fireweed, the slash would bequeath him nothing more than a scar.

The wound stung as Tresen applied a greenish paste with a familiar scent. 'Surely no need of sorren, Healer Tresen,' said Tierken. He enjoyed chipping away at Tresen's view of him as a *barbaric Terak Kutan* and took every opportunity to do so.

'I'm presuming your grandmother taught you it's best to use sorren when cleanliness can't be guaranteed,' said Tresen, busy with a fresh bandage.

'She did indeed,' said Tierken. 'I thank you for your aid, Healer Tresen.'

'The healing is given, Feailner,' said Tresen, as he finished up.

That was something else Kira said but her clanmate's careful courtesy hid considerable antagonism. *Does Allogrenia mean so little to you that you would give it all away for the scion of the brute Kasheron fled?* Tresen had demanded of Kira in Maraschin.

It was understandable Tresen did not want to lose his clanmate to the North. They were close and Tierken had intended to speak to him of Kira's time in Allogrenia, but things had moved too quickly and now he saw no reason to bother. Apart from Tresen's animosity likely tainting anything he said, Kira's life in Allogrenia was no longer relevant. As soon as the fighting was finished, he would marry her and she would make her home with him in Sarnia.

It was late when Tierken started from his sleep, scrambled up and set an arrow. He had no idea what had woken him but Poerin had taught him not to ignore the warnings his body sent and he scanned quickly. A mist had rolled in and Vardrin, Barid and Shird emerged from the gloom, arrows set too. The Tremen, Illians and Kirs still slept, and Tierken was reminded of Poerin's claim that Terak's sensed with their skins.

'A nice blanket to hide the stinking Shargh,' whispered Vardrin.

By Irid! The Shargh could have marked their fires before the mist came down! Tierken swung back to the sleeping men. 'Get up! Get up! Disperse!' he shouted. 'Keep your backs to the fires!'

There was a mad scrabble from sleeping-sheets as his men obeyed and Tierken peered into the darkness. All was quiet, and he had started to feel foolish when the air whispered, and he ducked. Spears rained down and he bawled more orders as he ran forward. He loosed arrows as screams and grunts erupted around him, but the mist scattered sound and he had no idea whether the Shargh were in front or behind. 'Keep moving! Keep moving!' he yelled into the darkness.

Now they had quit the fires, they were no more vulnerable than the Shargh but that did not make them safe. The squeal of metal told him there was a battle to his left but when he went that way he found nothing. He crept on, expecting a spear or blade in the back at any moment and, as dawn neared, the mist silvered and streamered away.

He was thirty lengths from camp and while Kalos grazed peacefully with the other tethered horses, dark shapes littered the grass. Tierken trained arrows on the

Shargh as he approached but they were dead. He wondered how many of their own men had been lost and was almost back to the camp when Vardrin strode out to meet him, grim-faced. 'How many?' asked Tierken.

'One,' said Vardrin.

One too many, thought Tierken, but he was relieved. It had been a mistake to let their fires burn into the night. Vardrin fell into step beside him but Tierken kept his gaze on the body ahead. The spear had caught the man full in the chest and brought a swift death. Tresen knelt beside him but strode away as Tierken approached, and then Tierken understood why. The dead man was Pekrash.

2

Three days of heavy rain in Sarnia had left the Domain's gutters full of rushing water and Kira full of frustration. She should be recording her healing but all she could think of were her neglected leadership duties in Maraschin and Allogrenia, her meagre supply of fireweed, and Sarnia's lack of Haelen.

It was dusk before the rain dwindled to occasional drips and she tossed on her cape and set off down the Domain path. The gloomy evening kept others indoors, which suited her, but the Guard followed as they always did. A breeze brought scents of wet-grass from beyond the wall and she raised her face and breathed them in. They reminded her of being out with the patrols, of how they sang lay-links under the stars, and of Tierken's face, lit by the fire-flames.

She quickened her pace to counter the ache of longing. It was a mistake to think of him, or Caledon, or Tresen. They could all be dead for many days before any messenger reached the Domain and the fear they *were* dead, was never far away, nor was the despair it threatened, and despair would not save the wounded.

The stables still smelled faintly of horse-droppings but men had worked through the wet weather to scrub the walls and floors clean. She paced past the empty stalls, her boots rasping over the stone, as she planned how pallets and shelves could be fitted. The Tain Sanctum had different rooms to separate the battle-wounded from those with more common ailments, but it would not be necessary here. Apparently Sarnia's citizens suffered no cuts, burns, broken bones, chills, or ill-birthing babes!

There was still much to be done but at least she had made a start. She came back out into the wet evening air in time to see a horse gallop past up to the Domain. The stables opposite were crowded with horses that she guessed were the messenger's escort. She quickened her steps and arrived in the Domain to see Laryia and Farid in conversation with a travel-stained patrolman.

They looked sombre and Kira's heart began an uneven thump. 'Is it Tierken?' she asked.

'Yes,' said Laryia.

'Is he dead?'

'No, nothing like that,' said Laryia, and glanced at the nearby servers who swept water from the paving. 'Let's go to my rooms.'

Kira held her silence until the door had shut behind them but her heart had migrated to her throat. Maybe it was Caledon or Tresen who had been killed. 'Tierken is well,' said Laryia quickly, 'and the other leaders and your clanmate. They were near the Azurcades but the messenger took eight days to get here, with rain all the way, so they might be further north by now. The message isn't only about the fighting, Kira, it's—' She cleared her throat. 'As you know, Farid must inform Tierken of all matters that concern the city's administration. He must—'

'Tierken's forbidden the Haelen, hasn't he?'

'He's refused permission to trade for it, which amounts to the same thing. I'm sorry, Kira.'

'Not as sorry as the dying men will be! Stinking heartrot, Laryia! Does he think the wounded can go all the way to Kessom on bearers?'

Laryia winced and Kira gulped down air. 'I beg your pardon, Laryia, I know the fault's not yours but I won't stand by and watch the wounded die. If the Terak Feailner won't trade to save them, then the Tremen Feailner will!'

'What mean you?'

'Tierken hasn't actually *forbidden* the Haelen, has he?'

'No.'

'Then *I'll* trade for it. I have the bracelet he gave me at Mid-market.'

'That was a gift!'

'So mine to trade.'

Laryia shook her head. 'Not the bracelet.'

'Well, the mare then.'

'You can't! She's a full sister to Kalos and Chime, and that bloodline stays in our family.'

'Then have her back. I don't want *anything* that belongs to *your* family!'

'Please, Kira . . .'

'Very well. I'll go to the Caru Quarter and trade myself. How much do you think the *Feailner's woman* will fetch?'

'Kira!'

'It's all I have left,' she said and stormed from the room.

The Tain troopsmen were growing restless. Four days of races, wrestling matches and challenges in arrow skill on the Baia Plain could not hide that the Terak and Tremen fighters were overdue. The weather had been foul so Caledon knew the chances of them being delayed by storms were equal to those of attack but time still dragged.

The sun was setting on yet another long day of waiting when scouts finally reported their approach. The Terak

Feailner's stallion emerged from the evening haze first, followed by the Tremen on foot and the mounted Terak. The Terak Feailner led both forces and Caledon exchanged glances with Adris as the men grimly set camp.

It was completely dark before the Feailner joined them at their fire. Caledon rose and bowed. 'Welcome, Feailner,' he said, and Tierken acknowledged him with a nod and returned Adris's bow. 'Forgive our lateness,' he said briefly. 'The Tremen Commander was killed several days ago and we diverted to Yelin Grove for his rites.'

Caledon's thoughts raced as he considered the consequences of Pekrash's death. 'How did he die?' he asked.

'A Shargh spear.'

'Come and eat,' said Adris. 'You've had a worse time of it than us. Meros be praised, we've suffered no losses.'

'Pekrash was one of two Tremen who *didn't* volunteer,' said Caledon slowly. 'The other is Healer Arlen. We needed a Commander and a second Healer. I thank you for Pekrash's burial near trees, Feailner. It was one of the few requests the Tremen Clancouncil made. The Tremen believe trees draw up the dead so that they live on. They say their voices can be heard in the whisper of leaves.'

Tierken shrugged. 'I know little of Tremen customs. Yelin Grove shortened the journey for the messengers I sent to Sarnia.'

'It's hard to think who Kira will choose to replace Pekrash,' said Caledon as he contemplated the Tremen taking their meal.

'Most likely you, as she gifted you trust to bring her men from the forests.' Caledon looked at him sharply. Did the Northern Feailner imply he had already failed that trust?

24

'We won't know the Tremen leader's choice until well after the new moon,' said Adris briskly. 'With your leave, Feailner, we'll travel together until then and share command. We have the last of the herders with us to escort to Maraschin. Once they're delivered, we can ready ourselves for the drive north.'

Tarkenda shivered as shadows circled the ebis herds. The wolves were emboldened by the hunters' absence but Palansa and the young Chief would not hunger, nor would those loyal to them, thanks to Erlken and his blood-ties' hunting skills. But those whose blood-ties followed Arkendrin north rued the lack of spears to protect *their* animals.

A panicked ebis cow could drop her ebi early, and see it devoured in its birth-bag, or have it snatched from behind while she drove off wolves from the front. And if she must spend her time in agitated flight, her milk dwindled, leaving little for her young, and none for the cheese-maker.

The warriors had been gone for over a moon but it had taken far less time for the wolves to sense their long hunting was over. Tarkenda wondered how many moons would pass before the survivors straggled back. She had no doubt they would be few in number for the last Telling uncurled like the fingers of a dead hand and poisoned everything it touched.

The gold-eyed Healer had seen a setting sun and given she dwelt with the gold-eyed Northern Chief, gold had met gold and two halves become one. But that was not all that kept Tarkenda wakeful at night. It was only a matter of time before the tesat the warriors used on their flatswords failed and the victorious Northerners come south, and not to gloat. They would ensure the Shargh never again raised spears against them by slaughtering every last one of them at the Grounds.

Orbdargan lounged by the fire as he licked the meat juices from his fingers and contemplated the Cashgar Chief. For once Arkendrin looked content as did his *shadow*, Irdodun, crouched at his Chief's side like a scuttle-lizard. Orbdargan's belly was full and the fire-warmth pleasant so for once Irdodun did not irritate him.

They had set their camp north of the Braghans amid the charred remains of a Tain settlement. The Tain burned their own sorchas now, which saved the Shargh warriors the trouble, and had taken their herds north. It made no difference to the Shargh. The Ashmiri now provided them with meat as well as horses.

'The Northerners hide behind the southerners' walls,' said Yrshin, as he claimed more loti from the pan. 'We'll be at their grand northern city before they rouse from their beds.' The Soushargh's chin was greasy, his shirt buttons straining over his belly, and Orbdargan's lip curled.

'The scouts saw naught of them?' he asked.

'No, Weshargh Chief. A few run back and forth across the plain, carrying their Chief's words, but their warriors are south of us.'

'They think we're south too,' grunted Arkendrin. 'They've seen my warriors there.' He chewed noisily for a moment. 'The filthy Northerners forget these lands were once ours! They think only they know where shelter grows and water lies!'

'Thieves only recall *their* ownership,' agreed Orbdargan, reassured by the Cashgar Chief's vitriol. Arkendrin kept to himself and his refusal to ride increased the risks for everyone. Already the Cashgar warriors were being caught more often.

'If the Northerners *are* in the southern walled city, we're already two days ahead,' said Orbdargan. 'Their horses are swift but if we strike north now, they won't catch us. The Ashmiri Chief says the Northern city is fed by beasts and tree-fruit from its southern valley. Scour it clean and they'll starve.'

'Uthlin's knowing is useful,' said Yrshin, as he reached for more spiced sausage.

'The creature's there and I want it alive,' growled Arkendrin.

'Uthlin's given enough horses for us all to ride,' said Orbdargan. 'We can be north in seven or eight days and the creature in your hands before the full moon.'

Arkendrin's eyes gleamed in the firelight. 'It takes longer than that to starve a people out.'

Orbdargan leaned forward. 'But not to trade with the hungry. Uthlin says the Northerners have no love for yellow eyes either.'

'I'll not ride and nor will my warriors!' said Arkendrin. 'The Sky Chiefs punish those who dishonor them.'

'You've lost more warriors than the Soushargh,' retorted Yrshin.

Arkendrin fingered his dagger. 'The fighting's still young, Soushargh!'

'Wolves hunt alone as well as in packs,' said Orbdargan soothingly. 'Horses will take us swiftly, even before the Northern robbers know we've gone, but a spear's best thrown from the ground. Both will reclaim what's ours.'

Arkendrin still glowered at Yrshin and Orbdargan gripped his arm. 'We fight as *Shargh* to take back *Shargh* lands,' he hissed. 'Who cares the manner of the fight as long as it's Northern blood that flows?'

'The Sky Chiefs care,' growled Arkendrin, but his face eased.

3

Kira pushed the damp hair from her eyes and surveyed the Wastes. They looked even bleaker than she recalled. Maybe it was the rain. It made the weeds almost impossible to struggle through and when she did, it was to step in putrid waste. The Guards' displeasure was plain but Kira ignored them, having to concentrate on keeping her footing on the slick ground. The last thing she needed was to injure her half-mended ribs.

She picked her way down the last of the terraces and gingerly lowered herself onto the broken seat. It was wet like everything else but she had to sit. The pain in her ribs slowly dulled and she was able to look about. The greenery woke a longing for Allogrenia as intense as pain and she closed her eyes. She had traded it for a life here with Tierken but he was away fighting and might never return.

There was a rasp of swords being drawn and her eyes flew open. A man clambered down towards them, hood drawn close, weapons at his belt and Kira tensed but then he raised his head. It was the Keeper, Farid. 'Guard Second Daril and Guard Farsrin, wait on the second step,' he ordered.

The Guard bowed and moved off and Farid stopped in front of her. 'The Lady Laryia is distressed you're here,' he said curtly.

'It wasn't my intention to distress Laryia.'

'Nevertheless, you've done so, Lady.'

Kira sleeved the rain from her eyes. Farid was angry with her, which was unsurprising given his friendship with

Laryia. 'There's no need to call me *Lady*, Keeper. The Tremen don't use the title and I know from your father many in Sarnia don't consider me a *lady* anyway.'

'I call you *Lady* out of respect for the Feailner and as a courtesy to you.'

Kira snorted. 'I don't need *courtesy*, Keeper. I need herbs and a Haelen.'

'I'm bound to obey the Feailner like everyone else in his lands.'

'Not *everyone*, Keeper. I'm exeal. He has no authority over *me*.'

The silence was broken only by the drip of rain and she closed her eyes again. The air might hold the smell of rot, but it also held the scents of the green and growing, and it was the only place in Sarnia that did.

'Are you unwell, Lady?'

'Why would I possibly be unwell?' she muttered. 'Your wounded are going to die horrible, agonizing deaths but apparently *Sarnia has no need of Healing or welcomes it*!' Silence stretched again and Kira steadied. 'I don't often ask for help, Keeper, but I'm asking now. I'll even beg if that's what you want.'

'As Keeper of the Domain, I will aid you in whatever way I can,' he said stiffly. 'But I'm bound by the Feailner's orders.'

'The Feailner's orders don't *specifically* forbid a Haelen, do they?'

'No, Lady.'

'So, if *I* traded for a Haelen, it wouldn't be contrary to his orders but if *you* traded for a Haelen on Sarnia's behalf it would be.'

'That is correct, Lady.'

Kira chewed on her lip. Even if she managed to establish a Haelen, it would be useless without herbs. 'Tell me what you know of this place, Keeper.'

'It was originally a quarry,' he began methodically, 'where stone was retrieved for the city's building and paving. Afterwards, Queen Kiraon had the hole shaped into terraces, soil spread to create beds, and plantings brought from Kessom.'

'What plantings?' asked Kira sharply.

'There's a list in the Writing Store.'

'Can I see it?'

'Of course.' He paused. 'The Feailner has charged me with your care, Lady. Given the rain, we should return to the Domain.' Kira nodded and he helped her up and kept one hand on her arm and the other on his sword hilt until they had passed the taverns and gambling houses. He obviously did not trust the Guard, thought Kira sourly.

'Are there Writings on how Queen Kiraon's garden was destroyed?' she asked, as they walked.

'I think it's been neglected rather than *destroyed*,' said Farid. 'I've found no Writings on the garden other than the planting list, despite recently ordering the Store.'

At least Tierken had kept his pledge to have it sorted, thought Kira. 'Did you find anything about Kasheron's ring or the Sundering?' she asked.

'I'm not authorized to tell you, Lady.'

Kira grimaced. 'Has the Feailner told you who I am?'

'He's told me who you *claim* to be.'

Kira bit back a retort. Apart from having to obey the Feailner's orders, Farid was his friend and hardly likely to take her part. At least she had permission to look through the Writing Store, so whatever Farid had found, she should too, *unless* it had been destroyed.

Kira's excitement at the Writing Store's contents ebbed as soon as she opened the first sheaf. Like the Writings in the Warens, it held countless of pages of trivia for every useful fact. She had found nothing by sunset and was wondering where to find a lamp when Laryia appeared in the doorway, eyes dark in her pale face. 'It's cold in here,' she said. 'Come to my rooms.'

Laryia's rooms were deliciously warm, the fire dancing high in the grate making her chimes twinkle and flash. Kira had not realized how hungry she was till she saw the food on the table. 'Sit Kira, and eat,' said Laryia, and Kira did as she was bid. 'Woodwrights will meet you at the stables at dawn,' continued Laryia. 'Tell them what you want and they'll begin.'

Kira stopped in mid chew. 'But how did you trade for them?'

'I have a very generous brother who's traded many beautiful things for me over the seasons from Mid-market.'

'But . . . but they were gifts.'

'And so mine to trade,' said Laryia ironically.

Kira stood up and embraced her. 'I thank you,' she said thickly.

'There's no need to thank me,' said Laryia, a touch of steel in her voice. 'I might be Terak's seed but I'm the granddaughter of a Healer.'

The woodwrights turned out to be Illian and only one of them spoke Onespeak. He translated Kira's instructions to the others, who discussed them in Illian before they asked questions which had to be translated into Onespeak. It was a tedious process that tested Kira's patience but it was important the Haelen be constructed correctly.

By the time she made her way back up the path to the Domain, a chill northern wind flapped her cape about her, and the Silvercades' peaks had disappeared under cloud. 'Irid likes to remind us in spring why we should be grateful to leave winter behind,' said Laryia, as they ate together in Laryia's rooms. 'Ryn predicts ten days of rain and snow and he's as weather-wise as any Kir.'

'It will be hard on the plain,' said Kira, hating to think of the men out in the open. The forests protected Allogrenia from weather extremes and the Tremen had never endured strong winds or snow.

'Don't fret, Kira. Tierken knows where the best shelter is,' said Laryia.

Kira woke to rain that gusted across the square followed by sleet, then snow, then more rain. It went on day and night, the wind howling like the wolves of Ember Keep. Kira used the time to search for the list of Queen Kiraon's plantings and, as the Store had no fireplace, took armfuls of Writings back to her rooms and spread them out in front of the fire there.

She worked through them methodically and learned much of Sarnia's early days and of the Sundering. There had been terrible grief for those lost in the fighting, and that had fed the fury at Kasheron and his followers' *desertion*. Every Tremen knew why Kasheron had fled the North but now Kira learned how the Northerners had seen it.

Kira sat back on her heels and contemplated the fire. Everything had been so simple in Allogrenia. Healing, killing, the barbaric North, the healing south, but *nothing* was simple. She had killed to save Caledon and then come face to face with Terak's seed and fallen in love with him.

And now she was here, in the hated North, no longer knowing where she truly belonged.

Word came the woodwrights had finished at the stables but despite her excitement, Kira did not visit. Laryia had asked her to stay inside until the weather improved and she did not want to upset Laryia yet again.

Kira had wanted to help with the trade for the Haelen's bedding and they had argued over the bracelet again. '*You* traded Tierken's gifts,' Kira had pointed out. 'It's no different.'

'It is utterly different,' Laryia had snapped. 'By putting the bracelet on your left wrist at Mid-market, Tierken pledged to you in the Kessomi way. You can't trade *any* pledge-bracelet let alone one gifted from a Feailner.'

Kira had stared at her in dismay. 'He had no right to do that!'

Laryia's response had been terse and to the point. 'Tierken's not afraid to show his love even if you are.'

Kira's antagonism flared even at the memory. She was not *afraid* to show her love but the price of that love was a lot more than a bracelet. Tierken demanded she tie herself to him regardless of what might come and, as the Northern Feailner, his home was in the North which meant she must relinquish *her* home in Allogrenia, those she loved there, and the leadership. She had never sought the leadership but renouncing it meant withdrawing her healing from the Tremen, which contradicted *everything* she had fought for.

None of it mattered at the moment anyway, she reminded herself, as she opened the next sheaf. For somewhere, buried in the pile of Writings she had yet to read, was a list of herbs that *might* still grow in the Wastes and which, if they included fireweed, *might* still save Terak lives.

The wind dropped so suddenly on the tenth night that Kira woke. How could anyone predict the weather so accurately? she wondered. She curled into a ball, snug beneath the covers, but all she could think of was Tierken, Caledon and Tresen out on the frigid plain.

She dressed quickly, grabbed her pack, and hurried across the square to the Domain gate. It was still dark, and the Guard swiveled as she passed. 'One moment, Lady,' one called, but Kira strode on.

The moon was small and no lamplight escaped the shuttered windows but not everyone in Sarnia slept. There was movement at the stables opposite the Haelen, patrol lately come in and still mounted. 'Gently there, Barid. That's it. Now Ralin, the bone-setter's in the south-west Illian Quarter, you say?'

It was Jonred and Kira hurried over in time to see a patrolman lifted from the back of a horse. 'Patrol Leader Jonred. Let me see him.'

Jonred swiveled. 'You had news of our arrival, Lady?' he asked in surprise.

'No. Bring him this way and get a lamp from the stables,' ordered Kira.

It was freezing in the Haelen, pitch-black, and full of the smell of new cut-wood. Kira fumbled her way forward and skinned her knuckles on an empty pallet as she searched for the newly-traded bedding. A patrolman held a lamp aloft behind her and the throw of light revealed the furthest pallet piled high with mattresses and covers. She grabbed a mattress, hardly aware of the Domain Guard helping her unroll it, and the injured man was lowered onto it.

'Shargh?' asked Kira, her gaze taking in his splinted arm.

'A fall,' said Jonred. 'The plain's wetter than a Caru woman's—' He cleared his throat and peered about. 'What have you done to the old stables, Lady?'

'Made them into a place to help the injured.'

'We need to take him to the bone-setter in the Illian Quarter.'

'Best he stays here,' said Kira as she gently probed his arm. 'You don't want to worsen his pain. What's his name?'

'Patrolman Sarim.'

Sarim shivered and Kira tucked a cover over him. 'We need a fire, Jonred, so Sarim will be more at ease, and we need fewer men in here.' Jonred barked orders and Kira turned back to Sarim and lowered her voice. 'I'm going to take the pain away then set your arm.'

The journey into the burning tunnel never got any easier and her cracked ribs did not help, and she struggled to hide her nausea as Jonred returned. 'His horse went down south of the Breshlin,' he said, his concerned gaze on Sarim.

'Is the horse all right?' asked Kira, as she brought the bones back into alignment.

'Yes,' said Jonred. 'How many breaks?'

'Three,' said Kira and Sarim groaned.

'It's his sword arm,' explained Jonred. 'He's left-handed.'

'It will mend the same.'

36

'More than one break, another living you'll make,' quoted Jonred.

'He'll have full use of his arm, Jonred.'

'That's not what the bone-setters say.'

'It's what the Healers *know*,' said Kira firmly. A fire had been set and already took the icy edge off the air but Kira fetched another cover anyway.

'I'll send men later to take him to his home, Lady,' said Jonred. 'We rest the horses for two days then return south.'

'I'll ensure the healing goes well,' said Kira. 'Do you know where the Tremen are?'

'The Feailner's message is for the Domain Keeper. I go to him now, for we've been much delayed by Sarim.' Jonred paused. 'It's a long journey from west of Mendor Spur.'

Mendor Spur! It was where the Tain men, women and children had been slaughtered. 'I thank you, Patrol Leader,' she said, and managed to smile but inside, she felt as cold as the Silvercades' snow.

4

Tierken, Caledon and Adris listened in tense silence to the final scout's report. It was the same as the earlier ones: the plain was empty of Shargh. 'Either they've gone north or turned east to Uthlin,' said Caledon.

Adris kicked at the charred bones in the derelict campfire in disgust. 'And judging by the filth they've left behind, they have a good two-day start on us. The Ashmiri Chief gifts them horses *and* meat, so comfortable lodgings will no doubt follow. What do you think, Feailner?'

Tierken's belly had churned since they had delivered the herders to Maraschin and now he understood why. *When in doubt, trust your guts; they're a long way from the excuses of your head*, Poerin had warned, but none of it made sense. The Shargh could not breach Sarnia's walls so why go there? And then his blood ran cold. By Irid, they did not need to!

'They plan to burn out the Rehan Valley,' he said quickly. 'It's Sarnia's main food source.' Had the Shargh's murderous attacks been a ploy to draw his men south, *away* from their own lands? And even with Kalos's speed and endurance, he could not catch them now!

'We must split our strength!' exclaimed Caledon. 'With your leave, Feailner, take those with the swiftest horses north. Delay the Shargh until King Adris arrives with the rest of the mounted men. I'll bring the remainder on foot. If the Shargh *have* gone east, the threat's delayed not destroyed. They'll force Uthlin to choose between blood and honor and I'll not wager on the outcome.'

Tierken galloped north with his best fighters and the King's Guard. They rode through the day and freezing night, stopped at dawn to rest the horses and snatch sleep, and sped on. The Shargh were easy to track; cold campfires, burned bones, and an Ashmiri pony with a fractured leg. Their quarry avoided the slopes and stonelands but Tierken's men could not afford to. They went in silence: the Terak knowing what was at risk, the Tain having seen The Westlans burn.

They reached Cover-cape Crest at dusk on the fourth day. 'They're a day ahead, Feailner,' said Vardrin, as he tested the fire-ash with his boot. Tierken knew it was a day that could mean slaughter in the Rehan, but his men must rest and so must the horses.

He ordered them to set camp and the men tossed down their sleeping-sheets and crawled into them but Tierken remained standing. The Tallien had been right; the fighting *would* be in the North. He should have understood what the Shargh's long hatred meant but had let his dislike of the Tallien cloud his judgement and the consequences could prove fatal.

He turned at Vardrin's approach. 'Derkash says the weather changes, Feailner. He smells snow.'

Tierken's heart leapt. Derkash was Kir and weather-wisdom flowed in Kir veins. Tierken's half-Kir mother had told him Kir herders took careful note of things that stole the food from their bellies. A storm could take half a herd in a day and wolves the other half. Snow would slow the Shargh and his men would make up time *until* the snow slowed *them* then the gap would widen again *unless* Irid sent wind too and then the Shargh must seek shelter. The nearest was Ember Keep and his neck muscles roped. The Shargh would be safe there from the weather *and* from them.

He resisted the urge to wrench Derkash from his sleeping-sheet and demand more information. The most a Kir could offer was to speak of *feeling* frost, *smelling* snow, and *seeing* cloud, even when the skies were empty. Tierken would just have to wait. It did not matter. Nothing mattered except stopping the Shargh from reaching the Rehan.

Kira supervised Sarim's move to his kin's house later that day and then went back to the Wastes. The rains had made the terraces even more treacherous but she could not afford to delay her search for fireweed. A Haelen without it could not save *anyone* with a Shargh wound.

Layria had sent to Kessom for herbs, and a good supply now hung drying in the Haelen's Herbery, and the Haelen's shelves were stacked with wash bowls, cloths, bandages, stitch-weed, lamps, lamp oil, flints and burning wood, which brough her some comfort.

The Wastes did too. Kira liked their lush greenery, despite the filth from the taverns and gambling houses, and she realized in surprise that if Sarnia's stone was broken with greenery she might even be happy here.

She narrowed her eyes as she tried to imagine what the Wastes had once been like. The air would have been full of spice from the alwaysgreen at the bottom, and the terraces fragrant with herbs and bright with their blooms.

There would have been birds too and their songs, and brightwings maybe, and moon moths at night, and perhaps the mira kiraon and other owls had visited from Kessom. And it could be like that again *if* Sarnia accepted healing.

'Lady!' It was Guard Leader Tharin, on the terrace above. 'The Keeper requests your presence in the Meeting Hall.' Stinking heartrot! It was her first chance in more than ten days to search for fireweed. She stayed where she was, tempted to ignore the summons. '*Immediately*, Lady,' said Tharin, his voice hard-edged.

Kira cursed under her breath as she picked her way back up the terraces. Maybe Farid had discovered just how many precious things Laryia had traded for the Haelen. She reached the Domain and her mouth dried as she saw Ryn rubbing down a mud-spattered horse. The summons was something more serious than trade, she realized, as she hastened across the square.

Farid and Laryia waited with a messenger in the Meeting Hall. He was white-faced with weariness but bowed and offered Kira a leather cylinder. 'The Feailner of the Terak Kirillian sends message to the Feailner of the Tremen,' he said formally. 'He requests the Tremen Feailner's response be returned with me. My escort leaves at dawn, two days hence.'

He bowed again and the door closed behind him but Kira made no move to open the cylinder. Obviously Tierken was alive but it could only mean someone important to her had been wounded *or killed*. 'You don't have to open it now,' said Laryia, her face full of sympathy.

'With respect, Lady, you do,' said Farid. 'If there's something the Feailner requires, preparations must be made.'

Kira slid out the single sheet of paper, read it, and sat heavily. 'Tremen Commander Pekrash is dead,' she whispered. 'The Feailner requests the name of his replacement.'

Laryia sat beside her and caught her hands. 'I'm so sorry, Kira.'

'I should name myself,' said Kira bitterly. 'I'm the Tremen Leader but I skulk behind Sarnia's walls and waste the lives of others.'

'No!' exclaimed Farid. 'You would risk *everyone*! The Shargh would use you against your people *and* against us. If you have *any* love for those who fight, you will remain here.' Kira and Laryia stared at him in astonishment. 'The Feailner and I discussed why the Shargh might hunt you, Lady,' he continued more calmly. 'While we can only guess at their exact motives, the Shargh believe the unusual to ill-omened. They would know from the Ashmiri you are with the Northern Feailner, and consider the joining of gold eyes to portend misfortune.'

Kira flinched as she recalled the Shargh's dagger poised above her eyes. 'They didn't kill me when they had me last time,' she managed to say.

'You are more use to them alive,' said Farid bluntly, echoing Tierken's earlier words to her. 'Alive, they can use you to extract all sorts of concessions from your people and ours. The Feailner would trade his own life before giving yours.'

There was a strained silence, and Farid bowed. 'Perhaps I've said more than I should or less courteously than required and, if so, I beg your pardon now, Lady, and I'll beg the Feailner's on his return. In the meantime, it's vital you remain here—for all our sakes.'

Kira made several attempts that night and the next morning to compose a message, but she had no idea who to appoint as Commander, or how to write it. Tierken's message had been brief and impersonal: *The Terak Feailner regrets to inform the Tremen Feailner that Commander Pekrash has been lost in battle. The Terak Feailner requests the name of the new Tremen Commander.*

He had said nothing about prohibiting the Haelen, or missing her, or loving her. In fact, the more she considered their time together, the more uncertain it became. She remembered their arguments more clearly than any words of love and although Tierken had twice asked her to marry him, he had refused to bond.

She grimaced and picked up her pen again. *The Tremen Feailner asks that . . .* Stinking heart-rot! Must she spend her life *asking* the Terak Feailner for things, hanging on *his* permission, living *her* life according to *his* commands?

Kira tossed down the pen, wrenched open the door, and strode out onto the balcony. The Owl Fountain tinkled below but she stared at the colored-glass window in the Meeting Hall's dome instead. The allogrenia and the running horse: one had its roots in the earth and the other was never still. Her lips thinned. How could she and Tierken ever be in accord? The window summed them up perfectly.

Yet Tierken loved her; she had seen it in his face but she had also seen his contempt for healing and his denial of Kasheron. Her knuckles whitened on the balustrade. He had asked the Tremen Feailner to name the new Commander of the Protector volunteers, but they were *his* people too, by virtue of the great Healer Queen, Kiraon, who had birthed Kasheron as well as Terak. She turned on her heel and went back inside. At last she knew what she must do.

43

Orbdargan scowled up at the sky as the wind whined and the snow thickened, and then wrenched his horse sideways to avoid colliding with Yrshin. The Soushargh Chief had stopped for some reason, and Orbdargan spat as the Soushargh warriors milled about them like leaderless ebis. Yrshin's need to fill his belly several times a day irritated Orbdargan but his failure to build the friendships needed to meld their warriors into a single force weakened them all.

'We need shelter,' said Yrshin, swatting at the snow as if it were blackflies.

'This is little compared to the Northern plains,' said Orbdargan. 'Snow can be thicker than sorcha walls there.' He rode on but Yrshin did not follow and he stopped again. 'The Ashmiri say storms travel quickly on the Sarsalin so it's likely clear ahead. We need to keep moving, Soushargh Chief. The filthy Northern robbers are likely on our heels.'

'Then the snow will catch them too then,' retorted Yrshin. 'There are caves west of here, big enough for horses. They have water and good shelter. We go there.'

Orbdargan cursed silently. It was bad enough to have the Cashgar Chief far to the south-west because he refused to ride without Yrshin going his own way too. 'I know those caves,' he said. 'If the Northerners catch us there, we'll be trapped like a scuttle-lizards in holes.'

'We won't be trapped, Weshargh. The Yaragars are high set and all three give good views.'

'Three? There are two, with a third collapsed,' said Orbdargan.

'There are three,' growled Yrshin. 'Your Weshargh knowing is poor.'

The snow thickened as they spoke and the Soushargh warriors muttered as their horses tossed their heads, infected by their riders' unease. Orbdargan nodded briefly; it would be dangerous to further dilute their strength. 'These must be different caves,' he said grudgingly. 'You lead, Soushargh Chief, as the Soushargh knowing is truer.'

They turned west and after a while the wind lessened and as the sky reappeared, Orbdargan urged his horse level with Yrshin's. 'The weather smiles on us once more, Soushargh Chief. We should turn north again.'

'*If* the weather is as you say, it will still be fine on the morrow,' said Yrshin.

'But we waste a day for no gain,' growled Orbdargan.

'*We*? *I* lead the Soushargh. Go north if you will, Weshargh Chief.'

'A third of our strength already lies behind us! Do the tales of our defeat in seasons past mean nothing to you?'

'Our forebears died with honor *in battle*,' retorted Yrshin. 'They didn't freeze to death.'

The Weshargh warriors waited in silence but the Soushargh warriors had formed a semi-circle around their Chief and Orbdargan bit back a retort. 'Our forebears also honored their blood-ties,' he said. 'If west is the way you would go, Soushargh Chief, your blood-ties go that way too.'

Yrshin made no reply, just urged his mount forward and Orbdargan allowed the gap widen before he followed. Let the mighty Soushargh go *swiftly* towards a snug bed in a stone sleeping-room; the *Weshargh* were in no rush to do the same, he thought sourly.

The wind strengthened and the snow thickened again as night closed in. Orbdargan wrapped his spare shirt around his frozen ears and then as wolf howls joined the wind's howl, ordered his men to ready their spears.

Yrshin had quickened his pace, the smudged outlines of the hindmost Soushargh now barely visible in front, and Orbdargan's anger increased. Did Yrshin think his mount could carry his bulk faster than a wolf ran? Wolf-wraiths flickered at the edges of his vision and he shouted warning and tightened his grip on his spear.

He had killed many wolves in his time but not in packs, and then his heart thundered as the howls were joined by the neighs of terrified horses and the screams of the Soushargh warriors. The pack had attacked! Orbdargan spurred his mount forward and then wrenched it to a stop as the dim outline of a Soushargh horse disappeared in front of him.

One moment it was there, and then it was gone. Orbdargan dashed the snow from his eyes and leaned forward. A second Soushargh horse staggered, its eyes wild as its hoofs gouged the snow, and then it disappeared too. There was a hiatus, and then its rider clawed his way back out of the darkness and lay gasping on the snow.

'Back!' screamed Orbdargan to his warriors. 'Get back!' Where in this filthy night were the Soushargh? *Where was Yrshin?*

'Form a circle, keep your faces outward, 'ware wolves!' he shouted, and jumped from his horse. He crept forward, stabbing at the snow in front of him with a spear. The snow had been churned to mush by the Soushargh but then Orbdargan's spear stabbed into air.

He groped around for a stone and tossed it forward but heard nothing but the howl of the wind. 'Yrshin!' he bawled with all his strength. Only the wind answered him and he stumbled back to his warriors.

There was blood on the snow, a dead wolf, and the remainder of Yrshin's warriors huddled in a group.

Orbdargan counted swiftly. Fifteen out of nearly two hundred! He wiped his mouth on the back of his hand. 'Are Yrshin's blood-ties amongst you?' he demanded.

The Soushargh warrior who had managed to clamber back gestured with a bloody hand. 'Chief Yrshin's sister-sons rode next to him and their blood-ties behind. There's no one else.' The wind moaned and the horses snorted and stamped.

'You ride under me now,' said Orbdargan. 'If the snow clears we camp. If not, we travel till dawn.' He headed east, deeming it safer to retrace their route than attempt a new one. The warriors followed in silence and he sifted through the bitter consequences of Yrshin's stupidity. They must delay their attack until the Cashgar caught up but even then, there might be too few of them. The Ashmiri said the Northern city was immense and that Northerners lived in the mountains at its back too.

He spat as he considered his ill fortune. He would need more than Ashmiri horses and supplies to scour the Northern thieves from Shargh lands; he would need Ashmiri spears. If any good came from this cursed night, it was that the Ashmiri's time of comfortable betrayal had finally come to an end.

5

The mounted Terak and King's Guard came to a halt, the men slumped in their saddles, their horses with their heads down. Tierken and Vardrin went on, leading their mounts, ignoring the wind's buffet as they kicked the snow aside in search of their quarry. 'Nothing, Feailner,' said Vardrin.

'No,' said Tierken and rubbed his neck. 'If they detoured to Ember Keep, we might be in front of them.'

'Or they might already have crossed the Breshlin.'

Tierken wondered morosely if Vardrin carried Illian blood as well as Terak. He had the same propensity as Marin to state unpalatable truths. 'We'll go on to the Breshlin. If they've crossed, they'll be evidence of it, unless Irid's sent snow there too.'

'And if they haven't crossed it?' asked Vardrin.

'Then Irid *and* Meros have blessed us and we'll have time to rest, send warning to Sarnia, and plan how to greet our visitors.'

They went on, finding no snow at the Breshlin and no sign of the Shargh. They splashed across the ford and set camp but Tierken rode on for a time, his gaze on the Silvercades. The peaks were clothed in cloud, but there was no sign of smoke. He yearned to reassure himself all was well in the Rehan, but that was two days away and Kalos too tired to carry him even one. He needed rest too.

The men not guarding already slept when he returned, Tain next to Terak, sleeping-sheets unfastened and weapons laid ready. Tierken found a place by the fire and gulped down the scalding cotzee Shird brewed for him. If only he knew for sure they were ahead of the Shargh! The Breshlin had crossing places further north, but steep-banked. It made the water deep and fast, and he doubted the Shargh would attempt them on the smaller Ashmiri horses.

He also thought it unlikely the Cashgar Shargh had reached the ford before them, given their apparent reluctance to ride, but even without the Cashgar, his men were vastly outnumbered. His breath hissed as he considered that Adris was a day behind and the Tallien at least another two. It meant he must deal with the Shargh alone.

The Tallien was right. Tierken must harry rather than fight them, all the way to the Rehan if necessary, slowing rather than stopping them until Adris and the Tallien caught up. The prospect galled him, but he refused to sacrifice men to a battle he could not win. He tossed the dregs of his cotzee into the fire and crawled into his sleeping-sheet, but it seemed only a moment later a hand jerked him awake.

It was Ayled. 'Horses, Feailner, from the north.'

By Irid! The Shargh had completed their bloody work in the Rehan and came back to finish *them* off! Then Ayled's lack of alarm penetrated his tired brain and he realized it was Jonred's escort returning from Sarnia.

'You've seen Shargh?' he demanded, before Jonred had time to dismount.

'No, Feailner. We had a horse down and a broken arm going north, but nothing amiss southward.'

'No sign of camps, Ashmiri horses, droppings?'

'None, Feailner.'

Tierken heaved a sigh of relief. 'The Shargh have run for the North, Jonred, and we've chased them since. Four days ago we were at Mendor Spur. King Adris is a day behind with the rest of the horsemen, the Lord Caledon at least two with those on foot.'

'Mendor Spur, Feailner?' breathed Jonred. 'Meros must have given you wings.'

'He sent snow, which was more use,' said Tierken wearily. 'We think we're ahead of them.'

'They're close?'

'Closer than King Adris and the Lord Caledon's forces. I need you in the North, Jonred, as swiftly as possible. I want the Rehan emptied, the people within the walls, and their animals close to the gate. And I want patrols at the Rehan's mouth. Sarnia must be prepared to take wounded too.'

'It is, Feailner.' Tierken stared at him blankly. 'The Lady Kira has had the east stables cleaned and weather-proofed, and there are beds and herbs.'

Tierken's jaw set. Kira had defied him *again* but why in Irid's name had Farid allowed her to? Rosham must be positively salivating at the opportunities the *breach in Terak tradition* opened up: the *new* Feailner's *lack of respect* for Terak ways; his *weakening* of the Sarnians' hardiness built through seasons of healing's absence; his covert *approval* of Kasheron's *desertion*, and subtler but more damaging to him *and* Kira, the suggestion the *new* Feailner had allowed his judgement to be clouded by the *pleasures* of the sleeping-room.

He could do nothing about it until the fighting was over but at least the wounded would not have to endure the difficult and painful journey to Kessom.

'I'll leave you half the escort, Feailner,' said Jonred.

'You'll need every man you can get.'

'No, Jonred. My orders *must* reach Sarnia. Pass them to Nordrin and Barid so if things go amiss, at least one of you should reach the Keeper. The battle won't be won or lost here; we'll slow the Shargh, not stop them. We need time, Jonred, and I'll trade for it as I must, but with *their* blood, not ours!' He clapped Jonred on the shoulder. 'I'll see you at the Rehan.'

Orbdargan set camp in the lee of a small rise so close to the Breshlin he could hear the river's flow but Orfedren's scouting had revealed the full cost of Yrshin's fatal blindness: the Northerners had overtaken him and held the ford.

Orfedren reported the number of horses equaled the number of men who slept or lounged around their fires, and if Yrshin had not robbed him of half his warriors, Orbdargan could have destroyed them easily. The Northerner's numbers now matched his and while he would still win any battle, the cost in warriors would be more than he could afford. He must either find another crossing or idle away his time until the Cashgar arrived and, while he delayed, the rest of the stinking Northerners would catch up. Whichever way he looked at it, the advantage had been lost.

Orbdargan spat and went to where Orfedren waited. 'Get the warriors up,' he ordered. 'We go south.'

'South?' echoed Orfedren in surprise.

'We'll find another crossing, turn east and remind Uthlin that Shargh blood flows in Ashmiri veins. The Cashgar can take care of the filthy thieves here and by the

51

time we return with Uthlin's warriors, nothing will stop our sweep north.'

It was close to dusk and Adris's men east of Cover-cape Crest when Nirthin galloped back to report the approach of Shargh warriors. Adris stared at him in disbelief. 'Mounted Shargh, on *this* side of the Breshlin, coming *south*?' he repeated.

'Coming south, King Adris,' said Nirthin.

'How many?'

'About ten patrols, mostly mounted. I didn't take exact numbers,' he added. 'I didn't want to be seen.'

Adris's thoughts raced. There had not been time for the Shargh to overrun the Northern Feailner and his men, complete their murderous work in the North, and turn south and, as the Shargh were on the *western* side of the Breshlin, the Feailner must have reached the ford first. It did not make sense. The Shargh would have slashed their way through *if* their intention had been to scour the Rehan Valley.

If Nirthin were right about their numbers, the Shargh must have split their force, although only Meros knew why. He cursed savagely. Well, he must deal with what he *did* know. For whatever reason, the Shargh came in his direction. 'How long?' he asked Nirthin.

'Close to dark, King Adris.'

The plain was stony here and the Breshlin more confined making it faster and deeper than at the ford. It provided a barrier against an easterly escape, especially in the dark and he silently thanked Meros for granting him time to prepare.

Tierken was on scout with Shird and Vardrin some distance from the ford when they came upon an abandoned campsite set in the cover of a small rise. The fire ash was still warm. 'The droppings suggest close to two hundred horses, Feailner,' said Vardrin as he returned from his inspection of the tether site. 'Their tracks go south.'

Tierken rubbed his stubbly jaw. Two hundred were far fewer than Adris suggested made up the combined Shargh forces, and after their swift travel north, why go south again? Maybe they had drawn off to the hillier land beyond Ember Keep, to tempt him to battle there, or else this was a diversion to lure him away so the bulk of the Shargh could use the ford.

They set off back to the Breshlin at an easy canter but Tierken felt anything but relaxed. *If* the Shargh had gone south, they would likely come across Adris or the Tallien. He hoped it was Adris because the Tremen were on foot, and for all their agility and skill, they were not battle-hardened. His thoughts swung to Kira. She had broken every Tremen tenet in asking Tremen to fight and he feared the effect on her of so many deaths.

By a curious coincidence he found Arnil waiting for him back at camp with a message cylinder from her. 'Any sign of Shargh?' he asked, as he opened the cylinder.

'The North seems clear of their foul presence, Feailner.'

Tierken nodded, his thoughts on who Kira had chosen as the Tremen's new commander and then, as something slid from the cylinder, he turned away. The Tremen ring of rulership sat in his palm, a small thing in itself, but a weighty challenge to his histories. In donning the ring, he not only assumed command of the Tremen but accepted Kira's kinship claim. His jaw clenched and he thrust the ring deep into his pocket then strode back to his men.

'Break camp,' he ordered. 'We go north.'

Tresen trudged beside his Tremen and Tain comrades, fear clothing him like another layer of grimy clothes. The plain was not as flat as it looked, with hollows that could hide dense patches of trees, or rank bogs, or Shargh. He had not realized how comforting the presence of the Tain King and the Terak Feailner's men had been until they had galloped away. They were big men, on big horses, who did not seem to fear anything.

According to the Lord Caledon, they were still two days south of the Breshlin Ford where the Tain King and Terak Feailner had gone and, although the march had been unrelenting, the weather had stayed fine and they had seen no Shargh.

Each day ended with the Lord Caledon reiterating his instructions on how to respond to mounted attacks but they only added to Tresen's dread. He saw Pekrash's face in his dreams, wide-eyed in death, and had grown used to waking in a sweat, in the same way he had grown used to eating meat.

There was barely enough time to trap and cook silverjacks now, let alone seek out nutgroves. Since Pekrash's death, fires were lit only for a short while and it made the nights long, chill and cheerless.

They set camp at dusk as usual and Tresen was contemplating yet another nauseating meal of meat when there was a scream and someone shoved him violently sideways. He was aware that a spear sliced past him and of a grunt of the man impaled behind, and then a Shargh filled his vision.

Tresen threw up his blade to block the sword slash, but the clash jarred the old wound to his shoulder and he stumbled backwards. The Shargh was on him in a flash, then gone, as a Tain sword slashed down. He was showered with blood but scrabbled upright, planted his feet, and focused on the next Shargh. His breath rasped as if he ran but he thought only of how to turn blades and blows aside before they reached him. He had no idea how long he endured it, but he finally had time to sleeve the sweat from his eyes and look around. He was shaking, his hands greasy with blood, and Tain and Tremen wounded littered the ground.

He needed to staunch the bleeding, use fireweed, stitch and bind, but first he needed his pack. He turned and then something smashed him in the back. It threw him onto his knees and he swayed there a moment, his gaze on blood that dripped to the ground. *His* blood, he realized in horror, and collapsed forward into oblivion.

Adris hid his men in a shallow dip, further from the river than he wanted, but keen to keep the element of surprise. He hoped the Shargh would not ride too close to the Breshlin but when they came into view, they hugged its bank. It meant his men would be seen before the Shargh were within arrow range but it could not be helped.

He counted swiftly as the Shargh advanced. About two hundred, as Nirthin had estimated. *If* they had slaughtered their way through the Feailner's force at the ford *and* plundered the Rehan Valley they would have paid a heavy price, but there were no wounded amongst them nor riderless horses.

Adris's knuckles whitened on the reins. *Whatever* had unfolded north, he would make sure few of the murdering brutes escaped to rejoin their comrades. The Shargh drew inexorably closer and he brought his arm down in a chopping motion and led his men in a great thundering sweep down from their hiding place. He expected the Shargh to launch their spears or take up defensive positions but chaos erupted.

Some fled north, others south, but most spurred their horses into the water and Adris struggled to comprehend what he saw. The river was full of men and horses swept downstream by the water's swift flow and he and his men galloped south along the bank, shooting those in the water.

Dead Shargh and horses bobbed along together while other panic-stricken horses fought to keep their heads above the flow or struggled up the bank to gallop riderless beside him. The first of the Shargh reached the far bank and Adris bawled warning, expecting a hail of spears, but the Shargh clambered back onto their sodden beasts and galloped east, *towards the Ashmiri.*

The sky was full of stars but Caledon had no time to seek their guidance or admire their beauty as he supervised the pyres. The stench of burning Tremen and Tain was the same but the effect on their comrades was utterly different. The Tain stood in a solemn circle around the flames as they farewelled the spirits of their dead friends but the Tremen huddled as far from the pyres as possible, backs turned, heads bowed.

The Tremen did not love Caledon for what he did but they did not hate him either. They understood burials took time and time cost the lives of the wounded. The Tremen had suffered more deaths than the Tain and more serious wounds. There were seven Tremen who must be carried, excluding Healer Tresen, who would not survive the night.

Arlen had done what he could but Tresen's face was the color of soiled snow and his breathing low. Caledon contemplated him grimly. He had come to know Miken in his time in Allogrenia and met Tenerini and Mikini, but his thoughts were on Kira. Now she would truly be alone.

Hoof beats sounded, and he whirled and drew his sword, even as his men scrambled to ready themselves for battle. But the horses that emerged from the darkness were wet and riderless, and as the Tain leapt forward to capture them, Caledon all but wept with relief. He brought his hand to his brow and stared skyward. 'Thank you, Aeris,' he muttered. 'Thank you.'

6

Kira could not afford to wait for the weather to improve to resume her search for fireweed. She told herself she had grown used to being cold and wet but it was a lie The terraces never got any easier to navigate and the Guards' disapproval never got any easier to bear.

They waited behind her, stony-faced as usual, as she surveyed the wind-swept weeds. At least Tierken had authorized trade for the Haelen, which told her the fighting came North, and that made the need for fireweed even more urgent. But her search had been interrupted by something other than the foul weather, something so unexpected it still astonished her: Sarnians had come to the Haelen to seek healing.

Kira had no idea whether her visits to Sarim's house to monitor his broken arm had alerted them to the possibility of cures for their own ills, but so many now came that Kira had to seek Laryia's help. Rosham might turn his back when she came upon him in the streets but in the end, like the Tain, Tremen and Kessomis, Sarnians wanted cures for those they loved.

Laryia's Healer skills surprised Kira too. Laryia had learned many from Eris but was quick to learn more and there was a quiet strength beneath her sweet exterior. She had circumvented Tierken's prohibition on trading for the Haelen and now proved herself a knowledgeable and clear-headed Healer.

Tierken's authorization made it easier to equip the Haelen, as did the *gifts* the Sarnians provided in return for healing. Kira left it to Laryia and the Keeper to deal with those; the notion of recompense for healing was still repugnant.

Kira pulled her cape close as ragged veils of rain joined the gusting winds, but the Guard remained stoically silent. They should be grateful they were not being soaked from the legs up as well as the head down, she thought sourly, as she pushed the sodden growth aside to harvest two strange plants. One had white flowers and the other orange, but neither were strongly-scented. They might be just pretty weeds, but she needed to check them against Queen Kiraon's list.

The rain grew heavier, but it was the failing light that finally drove her back to the Domain.

Niria had just finished setting the fire when Kira deposited her soggy harvest on the table. 'You've found bressil-white, Lady,' she said, fingering the white-flowered plant.

Kira dragged off her wet cape. 'You know it?'

'It's used to reduce fever. *Bressil* is an Illian word meaning *chill*.'

Kira's heart quickened at Niria's unexpected Healer knowing. 'Is *nasen* an Illian word too?' she asked, thinking of the other strange words on the list.

Niria nodded. 'There's no real Onespeak or Terak equivalent, but the leaves are used as a salve for cuts and scrapes. It's a pretty purple color.'

'And is this torch-flower?' asked Kira, picking up the orange blooms.

'Oh no, Lady.'

'Well, what does torch-flower look like then?'

'Why, like a flaming torch, especially when it's ripe.'

Kira sucked in breath. 'Where—' she began, but at that moment the door was flung open and Laryia and the Keeper appeared. Niria glanced at them, bowed, and left.

Laryia came forward and caught Kira's hands, her eyes huge in her pale face. 'Kira, I'm sorry, I'm so sorry.'

Kira's gaze jerked between her and the Keeper, and a macabre bargain began in her head. If the Terak gods granted her a single life, whose would she choose: Tierken, Caledon, or Tresen's? 'Who?' she whispered.

'Healer Tresen,' said the Keeper.

The room swayed and the Keeper lowered her onto a chair. Laryia crouched in front, still gripping her hands. 'He's at the Haelen, Kira.'

Kira stared at her in shock. 'He's *here*?'

'He's terribly wounded Kira. He can't be saved.'

Kira threw herself from the chair and fled. She took the steps two at a time, sprinted across the square and down the dark, rain-slicked Domain path. Sleet sliced her face and her ribs screamed as she reached the Haelen and slewed to a stop, chest heaving. Tresen lay motionless on a pallet, his face the color of wax.

'I'm sorry, Lady,' said Jonred, muddy and hollow-eyed. 'We traveled fast and without rest. The Feailner gave men to bring him. We've done what we could.'

Tresen had no pulse but Kira tore open his shirt and laid her hands on the cold skin of his chest. She expected empty blackness but found a torrent of fire instead. He was already engulfed and she fought her way in after him. Kandor was lost and she refused to lose Tresen too.

Either we're together in life, Tresen, or we're together in death. He turned, but there was no peace in his face and no beauty, just agony as the fire devoured him. His eyes met hers and she was burning too, and then, abruptly, she was no longer in the fiery tunnel, but nor was she in the Haelen, but somewhere grey, and shadowy, as if caught between.

Laryia and the Keeper were there, moving in the distance, rippling as if underwater, and then they were gone, leaving her utterly alone.

Laryia stood poised between the pallets of Kira, and Kira's clanmate *Healer Tresen*. Kira lay senseless but at least her pulse was normal whereas Tresen barely had a pulse at all. The Patrol Leader told her the Lord Caledon had sent Tresen north on captured Ashmiri horses and that his escort had found the Feailner who had transferred them to Terak horses that had brought them to Sarnia as fast as horse and rider could bear.

Tresen's survival still seemed impossible, despite what Kira had done, whatever that was. Tresen was only the second Tremen Laryia had seen and while he did not look like Kira, their build and fair skins were similar. His hair might be lighter too *if* it were not full of mud.

Laryia drew some water from the pan beside the fire and used a cloth to clean his face. It was a kind face rather than a handsome one, although he would be handsome if he had nice eyes. But he was filthy. Laryia fetched pillows and propped him on his side then eased him out of his blood-stained jacket and shirt. The bandage around his chest and back was rank with stale blood and new blood seeped through.

She glanced worriedly at the wound and then at Kira, but Kira's face was as white as Tresen's and she showed no signs of rousing. Laryia fetched more clean water, washed her hands and then peeled away the bandage. She braced herself but nothing could have prepared her for the wound's horror.

She had to cling to the pallet to stay upright and it suddenly seemed to her that all the tales of Terak's glorious victories were reduced to this: the blasted body of a single young man. Laryia wept as she cleaned the wound and was glad there were no witnesses. She left the pink paste intact but applied sorren where the raw flesh was exposed, then rebound the wound with a clean bandage.

She drew another pan of water and used a clean cloth to wash the sweat and dirt from Tresen's shoulders and belly and the mundane act of cleaning him calmed her. He was more slightly built than a Terak, although his shoulders and torso were well-muscled and, despite being calloused, his hands were almost as fine as Kira's. Like Kira too, he wore no rings and having seen the wound, Laryia at last understood Kira's aversion to metal.

Laryia did not remove his trousers, flushing slightly at the thought, but took off his boots and washed his feet. Then she tucked a second cover over him, fetched a chair, and settled between the pallets. It was very late and she longed to go to her bed in the Domain but Tresen and Kira needed to be watched, and there was no one else.

Kira had once said it was pointless having a Haelen without herbs, but as Laryia rested her head back against the wall, she realized it was pointless having a Haelen without helpers too. Rosham did his best to seed antagonism to the Haelen in all sorts of subtle ways but if the battles *did* come close to Sarnia, the Haelen would need to draw upon the full resources of the Domain, and that was something Rosham would not ignore.

Despite her best intentions, Layria slept, not waking until dawn and then horrified to see the cover over Tresen was absolutely still. She pushed the shutters wide with shaking hands to let in the early morning light, turned and gasped. Tresen's eyes were wide and staring. Then he blinked and she all but collapsed in relief.

'This can't be death,' he whispered. 'Death has no beauty and you are beautiful.'

'You're in the Terak Kirillian city of Sarnia, in our Haelen,' said Laryia. 'Are you in pain?'

'There's no pain in death,' he said, and closed his eyes.

'You're not in death,' said Laryia mechanically. 'You're in the Terak Kirillian city of Sarnia.'

Tresen made no response and she laid trembling fingers on his neck. His pulse was horribly weak but steady and she exhaled slowly. 'Thank you, Irid,' she whispered.

Laryia was in the Herbery and the sun well up when Farid returned. 'Surely you haven't been here all night?' he said.

'Where else? Kira must have someone with her since she's made herself ill in Tresen's saving and there's no one else.'

'*Tresen's saving?*' gasped Farid. 'Are you saying Tresen will live?'

'My heart hopes he will, for Kira's sake,' said Laryia, coming back out into the Haelen. In truth, Tresen looked closer to death than life, and the hope that had fired with his waking ebbed. Still, he had spoken and slept now rather than lay unconscious.

Farid's attention was on Kira. 'Has she woken?' he asked.

'No.'

'Tierken will be angered when he hears how she harmed herself.'

'I would prefer you didn't tell him. I don't want him distracted.'

'You know I must report what happens in Sarnia,' said Farid. 'And it's better he hears the truth from me rather than some twisted version from the gossips.'

'Tresen is the first of those who might arrive. If we receive more wounded, Kira and I are going to need help, Farid. We can salve and stitch but we'll need people to wash the injured and sit with them.'

Farid glanced at the open window and lowered his voice. 'Tierken's ordered those of the Rehan Valley into the city. He expects the fighting to be very close indeed.'

Laryia stared at him wide-eyed. 'The Rehan,' she breathed. 'We *must* have help, Farid!'

'Tierken's authorized the Haelen but not Domain servers to work here.'

'Only because he hasn't thought of it.' Laryia paused. 'The servers' role is to serve the Feailner's family. It doesn't have to be *within* the Domain's walls.'

'They are the *Domain* servers, Laryia.'

'Only because the Feailner and his family live there. If I were to fall and sprain my ankle on the Domain path, they would render me aid, wouldn't they?'

'Of course.'

'Well, I'm at the bottom of the Domain path, weary and hungry, and I require their aid!'

'I will instruct them to render it,' said Farid with a bow. 'But I must inform the Feailner.'

'Of course,' said Laryia. 'We're going to need a place to prepare food too, and somewhere for Kira and me to sleep, *and* for those who help us.'

'As the Haelen is now fully authorized, I can arrange that without sending message to the Feailner.' His gaze went to Kira again. 'Tell me when she wakes, Laryia. The Feailner needs to know that.'

Those of the Rehan started to arrive as the day faded to evening. Wagons rattled over Sarnia's paving, Guard shouted orders, children cried and men and women called to each other. They must be billeted throughout the city and their animals contained in the lee of the wall. It was a massive organizational task, but Laryia had no doubt Farid would accomplish it with his usual efficiency.

She could not imagine the Rehan Valley burning. She had enjoyed many rides along the Rehan and Steelwater Rivers, and through the valley's shady groves and orchards of fruiting trees. More worryingly, if the Rehan *were* attacked, it meant the Shargh were less than a day from the walls.

To distract herself from the terrifying thought, she reviewed what she knew of salving and stitching wounds, preventing fevers, setting bones, and ensuring the injured took water and food. She had grown helping Eris gather and minister and had prepared potions and pastes too, but not since she had been in Sarnia. Tierken had been forced to put aside his Kessomi ways and she had followed suit.

Now she wondered why she had accepted the prohibition so readily. Why should more women die birthing in Sarnia; more sufferers of broken bones continue their lives with crooked or weakened limbs; more children carry the scars of their scaldings and burnings into adulthood? Surely the people of Sarnia deserved to be cured as much as those of Kessom?

She went to the Herbery and scanned each pot and drying bunch, dredging her memory for their preparation and uses. She should offer Tresen beesblest, not just water, she realized in dismay, and quickly mixed a batch, but he looked so awful on her return, she had to touch his cheek to see if he still lived.

She settled back beside him, determined to remain awake this time to give him beesblest as soon as he roused. There was a second reason she stayed wakeful too. Her glimpse of his eyes had revealed them to be the deep brown of river pebbles seen through water, and she wanted to see them again.

Laryia was rewarded for her persistence by Tresen waking twice during the night. He did not speak but he took small sips of beesblest and Laryia allowed herself to imagine him hale again, laughing and joking with Kira.

The noise of those of the Rehan ebbed along with the light, but Laryia still heard the crowing of birds and bleat of herd animals corralled close to the wall. Servers brought food and lit the lamps, and she managed to doze, but still Kira did not wake.

Farid visited again and then sent Niria to sit with Kira and Tresen so that Laryia could return to the Domain to bathe, but when Kira still had not stirred by dawn, Laryia feared Farid would be sending Tierken a message of *her* death not Tresen's.

The sun was well risen and Laryia dozing in the chair when Kira finally roused. 'Is it late?' she croaked.

Laryia scrambled up. 'Thank Irid!' she exclaimed. 'How do you feel?' Kira's face was pale and her eyes dark.

'Is he dead?' asked Kira, her gaze on Tresen.

'He sleeps.'

'I don't believe you.'

'He sleeps, Kira. I changed the bandage and he's taken beesblest.' Kira's face remained blank and Laryia wondered just how ill she was.

'He might still die.'

'I don't think you'll allow that,' said Laryia unsteadily.

'I won't allow it without *me*. I don't have the strength to bring either of us back a second time.'

Laryia swallowed dryly. 'What is it you do when you take pain?'

'I don't know what I *do*. I find myself in a burning tunnel and there's a wall of flame at the end.'

'Does it hurt you, this tunnel?'

'It feels like I'm burning and I'm ill when I return, but the illness passes.'

Laryia caught Kira's hand. 'But it must injure you, Kira. You mustn't do it!'

Kira's dark eyes came to hers. 'Are you telling me to let Tresen die?'

'No!'

'Are you telling me to let the children of others die? Or their mothers and fathers, brothers and sisters?'

Laryia's eyes shone with tears. 'I'm frightened it might kill you,' she whispered.

'So am I,' said Kira, with a poor attempt at a smile.

There was a long pause and Laryia took a shuddering breath. 'But it doesn't have to be all one thing or all another, Kira. We have herbs to ease pain and Farid's sending servers to help. It means you can rest more.'

'If we're to have servers, we'll need more trade, won't we?'

'Not for the servers,' said Laryia firmly. 'Their role is to help the Feailner's family and, by extension, our guests. And as you're our guest, and Tresen's your kin, that includes him.'

7

Tierken set camp at the mouth of the Rehan Valley, relieved the evacuation was all but complete. Now all he had to do was wait for Adris and the Tallien to join him. His men certainly needed the rest and so did he after their desperate flight to the Breshlin Ford but he knew the Shargh would regroup too for their murderous assault on the Rehan and even on Sarnia itself.

He prowled up and down. He was less than a day's ride from Kira, the woman he intended to marry but he might as well be south of the Azurcades, for all the good it did him! His hands came to his hips as he considered how things had turned. He had known becoming Feailner meant producing an heir but on the few occasions he had contemplated finding a wife, he had imagined she would be the daughter of one of the trader leaders or of the Marken, or even a Kessomi girl he had played with as a child. The Tremen of the Southern Forests had been as unknown and alien to him as the longing that afflicted him now.

At least the fighting had allowed the Tremen to build honor, and the friendships forged with his own men would seed goodwill and acceptance of Kira in Sarnia. In fact, some friendships were so strong he predicted some Tremen volunteers would remain in the North. He certainly hoped so, for Kira's sake.

When the fighting was over, he would take her into the Silvercades, to the Kristlin and the Foaling Fields and have time together like other courting couples. He wanted to take things more slowly. Much of their discord stemmed from things happening out of order. He had known her body before he had come to know *her*. He wanted time to build trust so she would have no fear of marrying him and taking her rightful place by his side, as his consort, in the Domain.

It was another two days and after moonrise before Adris reached the Rehan with the remainder of the mounted men. There were noisy celebrations as the men reunited and Adris was pleased to be back with the Northern Feailner too. There had been no more Shargh sightings which strengthened his belief they sought aid from the Ashmiri.

He discussed his thoughts with the Northern Feailner as they ate, and as the night drew on, and ale was shared, Adris came to know more about the Terak he had heard only tales of and his liking for the Northern leader grew.

Tierken was glad of Adris's company too. They were close in age and the frustration Adris hinted at, as he struggled to defend his people against the Shargh after his ailing father had taken to his sleeping-room, reminded Tierken keenly of his hard road to the feailnership.

There had even been times in Kessom when Tierken had longed to be as carefree as his friends, rather than spending his days in harsh training and, as he watched the fire coals settle, he recalled the final time Poerin had taken him into the Silvercades.

Tierken had been exhausted from a five-day trek and an all-day run when Poerin had ordered him up Mintlin Peak. It had been dusk and snow clouds closing in and, for the first time in his life, Tierken had refused Poerin's order. He had expected the old warrior to add to the scars on his back but Poerin had smashed him across the face.

The blow had knocked him off his feet and bloodied his nose but he was up in a flash and involved in the most vicious fight of his life that had ended with his blade across Poerin's throat.

He'd had to fight the urge to slash down and had dragged himself off the older man and set off up the mountain. He remembered little of the journey, except he had wept as he had run, and it was dawn before he had staggered back and begged Poerin's forgiveness. Poerin had embraced Tierken long and hard and what had followed had been a friendship of equals. It had been a brutal lesson in self-discipline and respect and one Tierken had never forgotten.

He hefted more wood on the fire as Adris turned the conversation to the strange events at the Breshlin. 'Throwing themselves into the stinking river and then running like silverjacks,' he muttered, not for the first time.

'And their numbers half what Lord Caledon claimed,' murmured Tierken.

Adris's eyes flashed. 'I've known Caledon since I was a boy, Feailner, and I trust his judgement with my life.'

'Then the Weshargh and Soushargh must have split. Either they've had a falling out or they follow tactics known only to themselves.'

'Like drowning or freezing in the Breshlin.'

'Not risking warriors in smaller battles suggests they fight without the Soushargh,' said Tierken thoughtfully, 'although Irid only knows where *they* are.'

'Gone home?' suggested Adris dryly.

'If they have, they would have run up against Lord Caledon and the Tremen and, according to the scouts, Lord Caledon fought the *Cashgar* Shargh.'

'Caledon may have more news but we won't know for a few more days,' said Adris. 'It will be good to have our men together again.'

'Yes,' said Tierken. 'The final battle draws near.'

It was another five days before Caledon and the Tremen arrived, having been slowed by the injured, but the wait had given Adris and Tierken's forces time to rest and mend their bruised and wrenched muscles. Tierken had removed the bandage from his slashed leg at last and had thought of Tresen as he packed it away, his frustrations simmering again at being unable to comfort Kira over her clanmate's loss.

He sent the injured Tremen onto Sarnia at speed, pleased he could get them to help so quickly. Being close to the city meant they had access to fresh food and fresh patrolmen too, as well as swift messaging: the extra arrows and bows he requested, arriving early the next day.

The Tremen did not use arrows and that needed to change, given that fighting with knives and swords meant being close which increased the risk of injury. He just hoped there was time to give them rudimentary training before the Shargh attacked. The Cashgar were probably only a little further south but he guessed they would wait for the Weshargh *and* the Ashmiri.

The thought of the Ashmiri *oath-breakers* galled him and he already considered the retribution they would suffer once the fighting was over. The Tallien did not believe Uthlin would break his forefathers' oath but given the Ashmiri had granted the Shargh horses, meat and the use of their eyes, spears would surely follow. And if they did, his and Adris's men would be out-numbered and the outcome of the battle for the Rehan far bloodier and less certain.

Tierken had placed patrols in the valley's wooded sides in case the Soushargh *had* by-passed him, and in the Silvercades' foothills to protect Sarnia's back *and* Kessom, although he doubted Kessom was at risk.

Marin arrived later that day with messages from Farid and Tierken perused them swiftly, stopped and re-read them. 'Tresen lives?' he asked in astonishment.

'He did when the Domain Keeper prepared the messages, but it's said he's closer to death than life, despite what the Lady Kira did.'

'Which was?' demanded Tierken.

Marin shifted uncomfortably. 'Is it not in the message?'

'Tell me, Commander!'

Marin straightened and cleared his throat. 'Jonred delivered a corpse to the Haelen, Feailner, there was no doubt about that, and then the Lady Kira lays her hands on him and he breathes and color comes back into his face, but she lies as if dead, with no color in hers.'

Tierken stared down at the message cylinder and it was a long time before he spoke. 'And now?'

'Niria takes food to the Haelen each day for the Lady Kira does not leave her kin or the other wounded there. The Lady Kira barely speaks and her eyes are dark.'

'What else does Niria say, Marin?'

Marin moistened his lips. 'She says it's as if the Lady has lost all hope.'

Tierken's gaze swung northward. 'And yet Farid sends only that Kira has tired herself and Laryia sends nothing at all,' he muttered.

'Perhaps your sister prefers you keep your thoughts on the fighting,' said Marin. 'Shall I take a message back, Feailner?'

The silence stretched. 'On the morrow,' said Tierken eventually, his gaze still on the north. 'Get some food now, Marin, and rest.'

Tierken remained by the fire long after the Tallien and Adris had gone to their sleeping-sheets, considering everything he had read or been told about the Sundering. He sifted through what Poerin and Eris had said, Farid's discovery in the Writing Store, the Tallien's descriptions, and Kira's claims. And he thought about his time with her, of when he had first seen her on the plain, the Shargh's violent marks livid on her neck and wrists, and when he had last seen her in Maraschin, her eyes full of love for him, her face pale with the pain of her cracked ribs as she had walked away to heal others.

If only she were Terak, or Kir, or even Kessomi! If only there were not this complication of kinship claim! He grimaced knowing he must deal with what *was* and swiftly. He had seen for himself how her insistence on taking pain left her vulnerable to illness, and it was no surprise she had given her all to save her clanmate. But Tierken knew she would give her all to save *every* wounded patrolman, and there would be many of those before the fighting was finished.

To survive, she must have reason to look beyond the present darkness, to the day they would be together in love. In short, she must be given reason to hope. But in giving her that reason, he also gave Rosham a potent weapon to wield against him in his absence. His breath sifted through his teeth, as he considered his options. If he must risk what had cost him three hard years to build in Sarnia, so be it. He would just have to deal with the consequences of his decision when the fighting was over.

By the time the mist cleared the next morning, Tierken had dispatched Marin with a message to Farid, and ordered Jonred to assemble the Terak and Tremen on the flatter ground near the horses' tether-line. Adris and the Tallien were clearly puzzled, but Tierken said nothing to them, just strode out to address his men.

He took up position in front of them and glanced up at the dwinhirs that dipped and dived in the cloudless sky. Then he slipped on the ring and held his hand aloft. 'This is the ring of rulership the Northern Leaders long used to mark their sovereignty,' he said, his voice ringing out through the still morning air. 'It carries the galloping horse and allogrenia, mark of the Terak Kirillian and at the Sundering, of Prince Kasheron who, as the elder brother, took the ring with him when he left.

'Those of us who carry the blood of the peoples *Prince Terak* founded, tell bitter tales of that time. The Sundering broke our people and weakened us in our struggle against the Shargh.' The men were motionless, the Terak held by respect, the Tremen by the same tension that knotted Tierken's guts. 'Those of you who carry the blood of the peoples Kasheron founded also tell tales of that time, but very different to ours.

'I am indebted to the Lord Caledon, who has travelled many lands, both north and south, for sharing his knowing of *their* histories with me. I am also indebted to the Keeper

74

of the Domain, who made a thorough search of the Writings stored in Sarnia, Writings that Terak himself left behind.

'What the Keeper found confirms what the Lord Caledon discovered elsewhere, as does the return of this ring. Kasheron and his followers did *not* go north over the seas, as many tales tell, but south, to the forests beyond the Azurcades. There Kasheron established his own healing community that he named Allogrenia, and where he called his people the Tremen.'

There was a stunned silence followed by a wave of muttering. The claim was not new to the Terak, some had heard Kira make it in Maraschin, but to hear if from the Feailner's own mouth was another matter entirely. But Tierken had ordered Jonred to line-up Terak next to Tremen, and the friendships mitigated the shock and anger.

Tierken waited for the noise to ebb. 'It was the Shargh's brutality that sundered our peoples,' he said, his voice hard-edged, 'and it's their brutality that makes us whole again. This ring was brought north by the Tremen Leader, Feailner Kiraon of Kashclan—*Kasheron's clan*.'

Again discussion broke out, this time less raucously, as the Terak perceived how their Feailner's words fitted with those of Sarnia's gossips.

'Make no mistake that those of us who trace our blood back to Terak's people, and those of you who trace your blood back to Kasheron's, fight for the same things,' said Tierken grimly, 'but with fighting comes injury and death. The Tremen Leader is a skilled Healer and, even as we use swords and arrows to defeat the Shargh, the Tremen Leader uses healing to mend the injuries the Shargh inflict.' Tierken paused, and there was an uneasy silence as the Terak's antagonism to healing struggled with their natural wish to be cured of their hurts.

'The Shargh murder the Tremen and burn the Tremen's lands,' said Tierken more quietly. 'They murder the Tain of The Westlans and burn their settlements. They plan to murder the Terak Kirillian and burn *our* settlements. They would even burn Sarnia itself.

'The Shargh's hatred is long and will endure until they scour us from the lands. We will only defeat them if we fight with the Tain as one: the Terak, the Illians, the Kirs, the Kessomis *and* the Tremen for we *are* one.'

The men's faces showed only grim determination and Tierken nodded to the Patrol Leaders who marched them off for arrow training. Tierken watched them calmly, but he felt as if he had endured days of battle and it suddenly came to him that all the seasons of struggle to bind his men to his will had been for this precise moment, when he must force them to accept the other half of themselves.

He stared up at the circling dwinhir again. The dance of the dwinhir or the disappointment of the dwinhir? He cared less about the answer now than at any time since he had met Kira. All he cared was that he had given her reason to live.

8

Orbdargan kept his gaze on the Ashmiri Chief even as he gulped down his second bowl of spiced sherat. The sorcha's fire made the small space stifling but Orbdargan knew the Ashmiri Chief tested his strength and when Uthlin refilled his bowl, he drained it again. Let the great Ashmiri Chief see that Weshargh warriors were far hardier than Ashmiri warriors!

Uthlin had spoken only words of greeting and generalities about grazing, and Orbdargan grew increasingly impatient. The women who sat behind Uthlin, next to his high-ranking warriors, still showed no signs of leaving, despite he, Orfedren and Urugen having been there for some time.

They wore the black cheek dots of the Chief's family, and although one had a face as weather-beaten as Uthlin's, the other was young and very pretty. Her breasts strained the material of her shirt and Orbdargan's gaze went to her often, despite her returning his stares with eyes of stone. She would be less disdainful sprawled naked on his pelts, he thought with a smirk.

Orbdargan brought his gaze back to Uthlin as he sipped his fourth bowl of sherat. The Ashmiri Chief looked well past when he should have handed the circlet of chiefship to his son but the young warrior who sat to Uthlin's right was disfigured, with one side of his body ridged with scars that extended to the hand that rested near his dagger. Uthlin must be bitterly disappointed if *this* were his only seed, concluded Orbdagan contemptuously.

'You ride south and yet your enemy rides north,' said Uthlin abruptly.

'I ride south to seek you,' said Orbdargan, irritated Uthlin had broached the subject of his visit with the women present. 'To seek aid,' he added, as the silence stretched.

'The Soushargh went north with you, but not south, and your Cashgar brothers travel alone.'

'The Cashgar Chief goes north but refuses to ride, so travels slowly. He'll wait for me there.'

'Yrshin and his warriors wait there too?'

'They dwell with the Sky Chiefs,' said Orbdargan. 'We were caught by a northern snowstorm and Yrshin took his warriors west. I followed, so as not to break our strength. He led his warriors into a hole with no ending. Few escaped.'

Uthlin said nothing and again Orbdargan felt compelled to speak. 'Yrshin and his warrior's ascent to the Skylands weakens us. I seek aid,' he repeated.

'You have our horses, our food, and our knowing of what moves upon the tracts.'

'And I thank you for them but to kill the Northern thieves I need flatswords and spears, *and* the warriors to wield them. You are our *brothers*, Chief Uthlin. *Your* blood flows in our veins. We fight to take back what was stolen from *all* of us in seasons past. We were *all* robbed and must *all* fight to reclaim *our* lands!'

Again Uthlin said nothing but this time Orbdargan forced himself to wait. Uthlin's choice was clear: reclaim his honor or bow to the Northern robbers.

'We take our herds north,' growled Uthlin finally and his glare made it clear no more would be said.

Orbdargan stumbled out into the cooler air, Orfedren and Urugen hurrying in his wake. 'He aids our cause?'

asked Orfedren uncertainly, as Orbdargan swung himself clumsily into the saddle.

'They come north,' said Orbdargan and then threw back his head and laughed. 'Now we'll see the rivers run red with the blood of the filthy robbers instead!'

It was a fine day in Sarnia, as if spring had at last decided to stay. The Haelen's shutters were wide and a warm breeze stirred the wooden chimes Laryia had hung near Tresen's pallet. She sat beside him as she ground sorren, glancing at the chimes but mostly at him. She hoped the sound of *wooden* chimes reminded him of his home amongst the trees and helped him heal.

Kira appeared around the alcove's curtain, felt Tresen's pulse, and then briefly touched the chimes. 'Pretty,' she said, but her voice was dull and her face held no pleasure.

'You don't mind, do you?' asked Laryia.

Kira shook her head. 'But Tierken might think seven days insufficient time for you to give your heart to a man who does nothing but sleep.'

Laryia colored. 'I know it sounds foolish, Kira, but when Tresen opened his eyes, I knew he was the man I would marry.'

Kira stilled, reminded Tierken's words to her: *From that moment on the plain, when you raised your head, I've wanted you.* Even if such swift certainty in matters of the heart was a family trait, Tierken would never give permission for his sister to bond with the seed of the despised Kasheron.

'Tresen's not married, is he?' asked Laryia anxiously.

'The Tremen don't marry.'

'Bonded then.'

'No.'

'Is there someone in Allogrenia who waits for him? Who loves him?'

'There are many in Allogrenia who love him but I understand what you ask. Tresen courted before the attacks but turned away. I think the killing made him reluctant to risk his heart.'

Laryia gave a small smile. 'I should be sorry, but I'm not.'

She yawned and Kira eyed her. 'You're tired, Laryia. Go back to the Domain and rest. I'll sit with him.'

'I need to speak with Farid then I'll come back. You need to rest too.' She paused. 'Your eyes are still dark.'

Kira shrugged. 'My eyes have always changed color.'

Laryia gave her a hug and disappeared beyond the curtain and Kira settled on Laryia's seat. Kira knew her eyes mirrored the emptiness within, as if death had claimed something of her in compensation for her *reclaiming* of Tresen.

The spill of sunlight from the open shutters warmed her and the voices that drifted in were comforting. Mothers scolding children, men's deeper voices, and laughter; the sounds of people going about their normal, *uninjured,* lives.

She rested back against the wall and dozed, then started awake as something touched her. 'I didn't mean to startle you,' whispered Tresen. He'd had enough strength to reach out to her, realized Kira in surprise, as she poured him beesblest. He managed to drink some of it too. 'You came and got me,' he said in wonder. 'Did it hurt you?'

'You might still die, Tresen.'

'You won't let me.' His eyelids drooped and then fluttered open again. 'There was a woman . . .'

'With fine skin, dark hair and eyes?' Tresen nodded imperceptibly. 'The Lady Laryia, sister to the Terak Feailner,' said Kira. 'She's barely left your side but I've sent her back to the Domain to rest. That's where the Northern rulers live,' she added.

'Why?' whispered Tresen.

'Why do they live behind a second wall or why does Laryia sit by your pallet day and night?'

Tresen was too weak to respond and Kira squeezed his hand. 'Laryia can answer both questions herself but not now. Rest, clanmate,' she added softly.

Kira knew she had much to be grateful for in that Tresen still lived but fear over her lack of fireweed gnawed away at her. The Keeper said a major battle loomed and she knew that without fireweed, the wounded would die. How many would be the Tremen *she* had asked to volunteer? She did not even know who led them, given Tierken had probably refused the ring of rulership and its obligations. She pushed the hair from her eyes. She should have nominated Caledon as their Commander. At least *he* knew the truth of the Sundering.

The Haelen door opened and she heard a crying child. Healing those who sought aid also took time away from her search. She hauled herself up and paused to look down at Tresen. Two of Kasheron's *cowardly Healers* had slipped back into *Terak's* city and brought healing with them, she affirmed grimly. Then she kissed him on the forehead and hurried from the alcove.

The day turned out to be filled with splinters, scalds, misplaced axe-blows, coughs that would not stop, and odd rashes. Kira was aware of Laryia's return, of Niria bringing food and of the movement of servers. In the brief break between ministering to Sarnia's ailing and injured, Laryia also told her Farid had authorized more helpers.

Eris had said no place was entirely bereft of healing, including Sarnia, and that healing continued beyond closed doors, and so it turned out to be. The new helpers had useful skills but that the fact the Keeper had summoned them, added to Kira's dread.

It was dusk before she had a chance to stretch her legs outside. She would have liked to climb the steps to the walkway atop the wall and look out over the grasses of the Rehan Valley, but she dare not stray far from the Haelen. Tresen slept but Laryia had gone back to the Domain to speak to the Keeper.

Kira had loved dusk in Allogrenia when the brightwings and moon moths woke and the mira kiraon left its roost and flashed through the trees to hunt. It was beautiful on the plain too, where the grasses silvered as the skies filled with swirls of brilliant stars, but she could find neither beauty nor comfort in the chill set of Sarnia's stone. The houses turned inwards, as if excluding the stranger, and she was the stranger.

She could still hear the animals penned close to the wall, as she loitered near the Haelen, but they were quieter now, as if they prepared for night and then one of the massive wooden wall gates creaked open and a lone rider appeared. A messenger, by the look of him, who would gallop on up to the Domain but surprisingly, the rider turned in her direction instead.

It was Marin. 'Lady Kira,' he said, with a smile. 'This is good fortune. I come from the Feailner with a message for the Keeper but also for you. Is there somewhere we can speak?'

'In the Haelen,' said Kira, more calmly than she felt. No message from *the Feailner* would be good news. She led Marin past the pallets to the small space as the end where she and Laryia ate, took the pan from the fire and poured him a mug of cotzee.

He gulped it down and she poured him a second, and he finished that as well. 'You look better than expected,' he said as he eyed her.

'Should I take that as a compliment or as an insult, Commander?'

'A compliment,' said Marin with a grin.

'And Tierken? Is he well? And Caledon?'

'Both well,' said Marin. 'And the Feailner's leg is all healed.'

'His leg?'

'A nasty sword slash on the calf, early in the fighting. Healer Tresen stitched it up.'

Tresen was thorough but Kira longed to make sure the wound had healed cleanly, that no Shargh filth remained, that— Marin had stood and his expression made Kira's heart quicken.

'The Feailner ordered me to deliver this message to you, before I delivered his message to the Keeper,' said Marin, and cleared his throat. 'The Terak Feailner thanks the Tremen Feailner for the ring of rulership. He wears it now as a symbol of the long-sundered seed of Terak and Kasheron being united once more.

'He instructs the Keeper of the Domain to grant Kasheron's kin and the kin of his followers the rights and privileges accorded to all others of the Terak Kirillian peoples, and looks forward to the formal granting of Kasheron's Quarter to the Tremen Feailner's people on his return.'

Kira gaped at him, half-expecting Marin to break into uproarious laughter at his joke but his expression gentled instead. 'The Feailner's recognized your kinship claim, Lady. It's a cause of celebration for your people.'

'But not for yours,' said Kira slowly.

'It will be a hard thing for Sarnia to accept and the Marken won't help,' admitted Marin. 'Is there a message you would have me take back?'

Kira stared at the fire-coals' soft pulse. After the long struggle to gain Tierken's recognition, the victory felt hollow. The Tremen would die on the plains regardless and so would the Tain Troopsmen and the Terak patrolmen. They were *all* sons, brothers and bondmates; *all* loved.

Tierken might die too *and* Caledon and she clenched her hands to still their shaking. There was nothing to be said about the horror to come and she shook her head.

'I'll bid you a good night then,' said Marin.

9

Farid stood at the Meeting Hall window as the sun rose the next morning. He had carried out the Feailner's orders to the letter and now fended off his weariness with his third mug of cotzee as he waited for the inevitable. 'Right on time,' he muttered, as a figure moved swiftly over the square.

His father must have just received Tierken's declaration, which had been transcribed and delivered to all the Marken's houses, and Tierken's prediction of Rosham's reaction appeared to be eerily accurate.

I understand that my acceptance of the kinship claim by the descendants of Kasheron and his followers will cause consternation to some in Sarnia. I leave it to your considerable powers of persuasion to ensure the process of recognition and establishment of rights is carried out promptly and smoothly.

Farid's lips thinned. He was going to need more than *powers of persuasion.* He heard the staccato of footsteps in the hallway outside and then the door was flung open and his father stormed in. 'I require confirmation this is a mistake,' he said, thrusting the message-paper under Farid's nose.

'I cannot give you such confirmation.'

'Surely you're not saying that this act of . . . *treachery* is deliberate?'

'Take care with your words, father,' said Farid tightly.

'I knew the Feailner had taken a *liking* to this southern woman, but I hadn't realized the *pleasures* she afforded him were so seductive as to make him forget both his honor *and* his duty!'

'Father!'

Rosham slammed the message-paper onto the table. 'Do not pretend this decision is motivated by other than lust! You know as well as I do her claim is driven by her wish to insinuate her ragged tribe of tree-dwellers into the richness of our city.'

'You insult the Feailner and the Leader of the Tremen!'

'The *Leader of the Tremen*!' sneered Rosham. 'Do you know where the *Leader of the Tremen* is now? The *Feailner's woman*? In the Caru Quarter, where she belongs. No doubt she makes a tidy profit for herself while the Feailner's not present to grant her every whim!'

'Lord Rosham! You will retract those words immediately or be expelled from the city!' Laryia stood in the doorway, her face as hard as her voice.

Rosham gave a curt bow. 'I meant no insult to you, Lady Laryia.'

'Nevertheless, you *have* insulted me, *and* the Feailner, *and* the Lady Kira. You *will* retract your words or leave the city!'

'With respect, Lady, you do not have the authority to expel *anyone* from the city. Only the Feailner may do that.'

Laryia strode into the room. Farid had never seen her so angry nor so controlled. She had been only sixteen seasons when she had first come to Sarnia, a pretty, unsophisticated Kessomi girl who idolized her brother but who had since become the assured hostess of all ceremonial occasions and the skilled manager of the Domain's domestic affairs. But what Farid had not noticed until now was her determination and courage. She stood toe-to-toe with the Marken's most powerful member and stared him down.

'You are mistaken, *Lord* Rosham,' she said. 'In the Feailner's absence, the Feailner's family assumes authority of the Sarnia Guard.'

'The Lady Laryia is correct,' said Farid evenly. 'The Keeper of the Domain administers the city but the Feailner, or in his absence, the Feailner's kin, command the Guard.'

Rosham nodded stiffly. 'I withdraw my words and express regret for any perceived insult.'

It was a poor apology but Farid hoped Laryia accepted it. His father's expulsion would garner sympathy and make Tierken's edict even harder to enforce. Laryia inclined her head but did not drop her gaze, and nor did she move so that Rosham had to edge around her to exit the room.

His footsteps echoed away and Laryia slammed the door shut with a resounding bang. 'I'm sorry he's your father, Farid.'

'So am I at this moment.'

Laryia threw herself into a chair. 'It's going to be hard, isn't it? Few people will dare say what your father just did, but they will think it, won't they?'

'It won't be easy,' conceded Farid. 'No one remembers Kasheron and his folk fondly and our histories say he went north, over the oceans, never to return.'

'Did Tierken say why he's acknowledged the kin-link now? Last time we spoke he insisted any shared blood came from the time before we came together, when *all* peoples were exeal. It's odd that he's changed his mind.'

'He gave no reason,' said Farid, 'but I know Marin went to the Haelen first.'

Laryia looked at him sharply. 'Tierken sent a message to Kira too?'

'It appears so.'

Farid poured Laryia a cup of fruited water and one for himself. 'Marin said Kira looked better than the reports suggested. Has she recovered from healing Tresen?'

'She pretends she has but her eyes betray her. If she rested more it would help but she's at the Wastes again, looking for fireweed.' Laryia rose. 'And as only the servers who know little of healing are at the Haelen, I must return there.'

'So soon? I was hoping you would breakfast with me.'

'I'm sorry, Farid,' she said, already at the door. 'Maybe tomorrow.'

Kira rubbed her aching back as she surveyed the Wastes. Their greenery and scent of herbs usually comforted her, especially at dawn, when everything was fresh, but today she felt weary and discouraged. The Guards' faces showed their usual bored disapproval and Kira's irritation roused. 'Do either of you know where torch-flower might grow?' she demanded.

'The plant that gives a red dye?' asked one of them, whose name she had forgotten.

'I don't know,' said Kira, taken aback he had actually answered. 'Show me anyway.'

The Guard made his way down to her and probed at the growth with his sword. 'I played here as a boy, and we used the plant like swords. There was a broken pipe . . .'

'A pipe?'

'A water-pipe, my Lady. This was a garden once and pipes brought water to help the plants grow.' He bent suddenly and parted the mesh of rank growth. 'There, Lady.'

A fractured stone pipe sent out a seep of slimy water. 'Which way does it go?' she asked eagerly.

'I'm not sure.'

'If it were used to water plants, it would run along the terraces, wouldn't it?'

'It's buried, Lady. This is the only place you can see it.'

Kira tested the earth's sponginess with her heel, went forward a few paces, tested again, then dropped to her knees and scrabbled excitedly through the growth. Slime soaked through her trousers and a thorny tendril left a stinging trail across her cheek but she did not notice, for there, in a line of five or six protuberances, was fireweed. Tears started and closed her eyes.

'Torch-flower,' said the Guard over her shoulder. 'Is that the plant you looked for, Lady?'

'It is,' said Kira thickly as she harvested it. She straightened and, for the first time, stared him in the eye. 'This is going to save Terak, Tremen, and Tain lives.'

'My aunt uses it to dye cloth,' the other Guard offered.

'Your aunt harvests it *here*?' she asked, terrified the supply would be exhausted.

'Of course not! It's no place for a—' the Guard reddened. 'It grows all along the north wall.'

'In what season?' demanded Kira.

'Oh, in all seasons. My aunt only dyes cloth occasionally, but there's no shortage of it.'

Kira's thoughts whirred as she made her way back up the terraces. The northern wall would catch leaf litter blown from the Tiar Forests and the run of water from the Silvercades foothills. Why had she not thought of it before?

Her breath emptied in a long, slow sigh. Now Sarnia had a Haelen, a Herbery, a steady supply of herbs from Kessom, and fireweed, and hope stirred for the first time in countless days.

She considered the best ways to prepare and store it as she made her way back through the Caru Quarter. *If* there were a good supply, she could harvest it often and use it fresh. Most herbs were more potent fresh, especially if gathered before dawn, although she did not know if it were true of fireweed. She needed to visit the north wall to check it *did* grow there but first she must replenish her supply of fireweed *paste*.

She paused at the Domain gate aware she should bathe and change but also aware that wounded could arrive at any moment. Then the Domain gate was thrust open and Rosham strode out and for once, he did not turn his back on her. 'The *Lady* Kira,' he sneered as his cold eyes roamed over her, 'and looking rather dirty. But then it's hard to stay clean, isn't it, *Lady* Kira, given your activities in the Caru Quarter?'

Kira flushed but the Guards' faces remained impassive. Rosham was powerful and they would be unlikely to challenge him. She went to walk on, but Rosham stepped forward and blocked her way. He was not Shargh and could not hurt her but Kira cringed, expecting a blow.

The Guard drew their swords. 'Stand back!'

Rosham's glare swung to them. 'I am the *Lord* Rosham. Do not dare to—'

'Stand back or feel our swords!'

Passers-by gaped and, as Rosham bowed his head, Kira thought he had bowed to her but then a gob of spittle landed at her feet, and he strode off. A shocked murmur passed through the onlookers, but no one offered words of apology or comfort. The Guard sheathed their swords and Kira watched her feet start down the path towards the Haelen.

Raise your head, a voice inside demanded. *You are a Healer! You are Kasheron's seed. Raise your head!* But Kira could not raise her head. Rosham's hatred was like a corrosive fluid that filled the void left by Tresen's saving, and the fragile hope that had woken with the finding of fireweed, flickered and went out.

Tierken held Kalos steady, the big stallion restive, as they waited for battle. Adris was to his left, but Tierken kept his gaze on the Silvercades. He wished he were there, with Kira, but he was glad the bloody skirmishes at last came to a head. The Shargh were gathered beyond the western rise, and to the north, the Ashmiri waited too

'They'll join the fight only if they see us broken,' the Tallien had said, and he was right. The Ashmiri would maintain their honor whichever way things turned, concluded Tierken bitterly. The men's tension was palpable and Tierken rolled his shoulders. Adris's mount danced, as ready for battle as its rider, but all Tierken felt was a savage determination to obliterate the Shargh's threat once and for all.

Scouts shouted warning but there was no need, the sound of the Shargh horses like thunder. They came in a solid line, their riders shrieking, Shargh on foot streaming behind. Tierken and Adris's men shot arrows as spears sliced the air, then drew swords as the gap between them and the Shargh narrowed. But instead of spurring forward to meet the Shargh, at the last moment, they wrenched their horses aside.

The Shargh's momentum carried them through the Terak-Tain lines, and while Tierken and Adris's men slashed at them as they passed, they did not follow. Behind the lines of mounted Terak and Tain, and to the flanks, Tain on foot released a hail of arrows. Many found their marks but most of the mounted Shargh surged onwards up the Rehan Valley.

Led by Tierken and Adris, the mounted Terak and Tain spurred forward towards the Shargh on foot. There were close to two hundred to their fifty but on Adris's signal, they split their forces to form a swiftly moving circle around their enemy. The aim was not to overpower them but to drive them like herd animals. The Terak and Tain kept out of spear range but stayed close enough to pick targets, Tierken guiding Kalos with his knees as he shot arrow after arrow.

The moving circle of horsemen forced the Shargh west, back towards the Rehan River. As the Shargh grew more desperate, a wedge broke free and ran north after their comrades, but there were still close to a hundred and fifty in the encircled group by the time they neared the Rehan. The last few days of fine weather had speeded the Silvercades' snow-melt and the river roared along in its bed.

When Adris and Tierken's men were about twenty lengths from the river, they dissolved the circle into a line, drew their swords, and charged. The result was as the Tallien had predicted. Unaccustomed to facing a solid wall of screaming, sword-wielding men on horseback, the Shargh broke and ran. Some fled northward along the bank, but most were forced into the water, and the bank was soon empty of all but the dead and dying. The river would claim some but most would struggle ashore downstream, soaked with freezing water.

Tierken and Adris's men paused only to haul their own wounded onto horses before they sped north again. They stayed out of spear range of the Shargh who had broken along the banks or escaped the encirclement earlier, and the Terak and Tain who carried wounded kept east, but the main force streaked towards the Rehan Valley. Smoke already billowed from it; Shargh work, concluded Tierken grimly, not the Tallien's.

They swept past the initial clash and dead horses came into view. Tierken's men in the trees had targeted the Ashmiri horses which were easier to hit than their riders. Their slaughter not only forced the Shargh back onto the ground but sent a potent message to the Ashmiri who could ill afford to lose so many beasts.

Tierken and Adris's men galloped deeper into the Rehan but there were so many dead horses, or wounded riderless ones, they were forced to slow. Tierken kept his gaze on the pall of smoke, his guts so tight he could scarcely breathe. *If* their strategy were successful, the main Shargh force would soon come flying back but if not, the *entire* Rehan could burn.

Despite the carnage, he urged Kalos to greater speed and passed the first of the houses the Shargh had torched. The southern settlements had to be sacrificed to lure the Shargh to where the valley narrowed and the Tallien waited with the Tremen, Tain and Terak patrols led by Jonred. The fighting would fierce there as the Shargh strove to break through.

It had been a hard decision to send Tremen to where the carnage could be greatest, but they were experienced in fighting under trees and had the advantage of the rocky slopes at their backs. Trees had been felled to form a barricade as well, which the Tallien would ignite to terrorize the Shargh horses, but they would have to drive them back with arrows and swords too. And if the Tallien's men failed and the Shargh broke through, Tierken would have to chase the Shargh and their fiery destruction all the way to Sarnia.

Time seemed to slow, then a single horse bolted from the smoke and Adris brought it down with an arrow. An eerie silence descended and Tierken wrenched Kalos to a halt. The rest of the Terak and Tain caught up and formed a line across the valley but still nothing happened. The Tallien had failed, thought Tierken in panic, and then a stampede of wild-eyed horses pounded from the murk and he shouted in jubilation.

Again they jerked their horses clear at the last moment then spurred after the Shargh. The Tain and Tremen would follow to drive the unhorsed Shargh from the Rehan's mouth then guard the entrance under the Tallien's command. His and Adris's men would chase the mounted Shargh south until nightfall, and Jonred's men would follow, driving the Shargh on foot before them. Then a relentless tag-team of hunting would begin.

Jonred's men would chase and kill, while Tierken and Adris's men would rest and trap their food, and then they would change places. Day and night, the latter aided by torches, they would hound the Shargh south across the Sarsalin. There would be no rest for their quarry and no food.

And any who survived would be pursued beyond the Azurcades until hunger and exhaustion claimed them too.

10

The first of the wounded reached Sarnia just after nightfall, and they had scarcely been found pallets when the next wave arrived. Kira and Laryia cleaned and laved wounds with fireweed, stitched and bandaged, or set bones and dulled the shock of the injured with sickleseed. They worked through the night, aided by helpers.

Kira spoke only to instruct Laryia or the helpers, and it was dawn before there was enough of a lull for Laryia to return to the Domain. She found Farid asleep at the Meeting Hall's table, head on his arms, surrounded by message scrolls. Laryia slumped onto a chair beside him, picked up a piece of fruit and ate mechanically.

Farid stirred, his face pale against the dark stubble of his jaw. 'How goes it in the Haelen?'

'Twenty-three dead and forty-one wounded, half of whom might die.'

Farid picked up his mug and swigged down his cold cotzee. 'The fighting was ferocious in the Rehan,' he said grimly, 'but I think the worst is over. Tierken and the Tain King will push the Shargh south and the Lord Caledon hold the Rehan. You can expect more wounded until they're south of Cover-cape, then they'll go to Maraschin.'

'I don't know if I can stand any more wounded,' said Laryia thickly.

'You need rest. Go to your rooms and sleep.'

'I can't. Kira's alone in the Haelen.'

'Aren't there helpers?'

'Helpers aren't Healers, Farid, not like Kira. In fact, no one's like Kira. She doesn't fear the blood like I do, nor holding gaping wounds together to be stitched, nor . . .' Laryia's voiced cracked and Farid pulled her into his arms as she wept.

'Kira's seen all this before, in her own lands and in Maraschin,' he said, stroking Laryia's hair. 'She's more used to it, that's all.'

'I don't know how anyone could get *used to it*. Now I understand her hatred of metal,' sobbed Laryia.

'Without swords, we'd be slaughtered like the Tremen,' said Farid gently. Laryia's sobs quieted and she wiped her face. 'Does Healer Tresen continue to recover?' he asked.

'Yes, praise Irid.' She poured herself some cold cotzee and grimaced. 'Does Tierken ask after him?'

'Tierken asks after you and after Kira of course.' Farid glanced at her sideways. 'But I wonder whether I should speak of Healer Tresen now when I speak of you.'

'He's just one of the wounded, Farid. Would you name them all?'

'Perhaps I'll just speak of you then, for the time being,' he said and Laryia managed a smile. 'But we both know it's safest for Tierken that his mind stays on the fighting. I've no doubt Kira's welfare proves a distraction and I don't want to add concern for you as well.'

'He has nothing to fear for me. I know my own heart.'

'And Healer Tresen's?'

'I know that too.'

Farid picked up a message cylinder and turned it over in his hands. 'You also know that gossip flies swifter than the wind, and certainly swifter than my messages.'

'It will say nothing more than the Lady Laryia works in the Haelen with the Lady Kira, and that both labor in the care of the wounded. And it follows that when Healer Tresen is well enough to be moved, he will join his kin, the Lady Kira, in the Domain, and continue his recovery there.'

'That I *will* have to report,' said Farid.

'By all means, Domain Keeper,' said Laryia. 'I expect no less.'

Thunder rumbled across the Braghans but Tarkenda's thoughts were on Ormadon's news. Their ebis herds thinned, and while the wolf numbers had grown, the absence of gnawed skulls and torn hides suggested it was not just wolves that raided their herds but other warriors. There was hunger amongst the old and the join-wives and children of Arkendrin's followers that if left unchecked, would seed not just theft, but murder.

Rain pitted against the sorcha roof and quickly built until it drummed like ebis on the run. Tarkenda was glad of the rain. It washed the air clean of the funereal smoke that blew from beyond the Braghans, and from the stench of charred bones that rode upon its back. The Northerners also burned their dead but Tarkenda's visions told her it was not the Northerners' spirit-selves the flames loosed, but the Shargh's.

Palansa hoped Arkendrin's corpse was amongst those that burned and so did Tarkenda, despite having birthed him and nursed him at her breast. Her care was for the young Chief now, not for the one who would destroy him. But the Sky Chiefs had long favored Arkendrin over those who fought at his side, and there was nothing in her mother's heart that said her second son was dead.

The rain that sluiced off the sorchas drenched the northern foothills of the Braghans too, where Arkendrin had taken refuge under a tangle of shrubs. He hated the wall of trees that hemmed him in, the groaning branches, the stagnant air, but it hid him from the filthy horsemen. Behind him on the plain, the orange light of their torches drew inexorably closer, but he stayed put.

It was fitting that he, the true and rightful Chief, was now alone. Only *he* had the strength and courage to endure. One way or another, his blood-ties had failed him. Some like Irdodun, had thrown themselves into the water rather than face the stinking Northern horsemen while others, like the Weshargh Chief, had turned tail and galloped away to save their cowardly skins. But they were unlikely to escape. It had been clear the Sky Chiefs punished those who insulted them, since they had snatched the earth from beneath the Soushargh's feet.

The rain dwindled and Arkendrin strained into the darkness with his one functioning eye. Then, when the night remained quiet, he pulled a hunk of meat from his shirt, tore chunks off with his teeth, and swallowed them whole. The Grounds had smoked meats and cheeses, fresh meats roasted over warming fires, milk and sherat, and the softness of pelts and hides but to reclaim them, he must fill his belly and fuel his legs, and seek the Sky Chiefs' favor. He lay a portion of his precious meat on the ground to appease them, palmed his forehead, and staggered away into the shadows.

Kira lay on her pallet and stared up at the Haelen's wooden ceiling. It was quiet beyond the alcove's curtains but she dare not sleep because sleep meant seeing Kandor die again, sometimes at the Bough and sometimes in the fiery tunnel, and often now, as the flames consumed him, his face became Tierken's.

She knew the relentless taking of pain triggered the dreams, but since the wounded now endured a journey of close to four days to reach the Haelen, it was too late for sickleseed, or anything else, to douse their pain. And sometimes all Kira could offer was a peaceful death and that meant suffering the burning tunnel with them.

Laryia had said once their men were south of Cover-cape Crest, the wounded would go to Maraschin, but Kira could not recall *when* Laryia had said it. Night and day had blurred into an endless horror of taking of pain; cleaning, stitching and binding wounds; and holding young men as they died.

A door slammed and she forced herself upright as sounds of groaning penetrated the curtain. 'You're not telling me you've slept,' said Laryia, barely glancing up as she cut a putrid bandage from a man's thigh. A helper hovered with a bowl of water but Kira made no response, just brought her hands down over the man's chest. Fortunately, his pain was not severe and her stay in the tunnel mercifully brief. 'And don't pretend you've eaten either,' went on Laryia, poised with the fireweed while the helper washed the wound.

Laryia had grown adept at haranguing, as well as healing, thought Kira dully, as she slipped her hands under a second man's shirt. He looked Tremen but was probably Kessomi. The Tremen were safe with Caledon less than a day away *if* there were any such thing as safety.

A hand gripped her arm and it took Kira a moment to realize it was Laryia's. 'No more,' hissed Laryia.

'One more,' said Kira.

'No more!' Kira tried to shrug her off, but Laryia's grip was surprisingly strong as she dragged Kira out of the helper's earshot. 'Have you seen yourself of late, Kira? No, I know you haven't. You haven't left the Haelen since this began. That's almost a moon, Kira! You barely eat and I know you don't sleep, and this taking of pain . . .' Kira managed to focus on Laryia's face. It looked different, more honed, her eyes darker against her flawless skin. 'Are you listening, Kira?'

'One more,' repeated Kira.

'Only if you agree to go back to the Domain and rest—for at least three days.'

Kira nodded because it was easier to let her head fall backwards and forwards than move it from side to side. The wounded man was almost at the tunnel's end and Kira fought the urge to journey on past him into death. Kandor was there, and rest and peace, but her Healer self roused and dragged her sweating and shaking back to the Haelen.

She became aware that Laryia held her upright with one hand while she juggled a cup of beesblest with the other. 'Drink,' she ordered and Kira gulped the mixture down. 'Now up to the Domain,' said Laryia firmly.

Kira retrieved her pack, came out of the Haelen into the sunshine and blinked. Things were too bright, as if the sky had lost a layer of skin. The Domain path seemed steeper and longer too. She watched the movement of her feet and saw other feet disappear to either side, like water that flowed around a rock. The bottom of the Domain gate came into view, swung open, and clanged shut behind her, and she raised her head.

The Silvercades gleamed, brilliant against a blue sky and memories of Eris surged back, and of Eris's farewell: *You know where I am if you need me.* Kira stumbled towards the stables. Her mare was there and she heaved on the saddle, and watched her hands buckle the harness. Then she was mounted and back at the Domain gate without knowing how she had got there.

'Where would you go, Lady?' asked one of the Guard.

'Kessom.'

'It's a full day's ride, Lady, and past the day's mid point. Glass Gorge is likely flooded too.'

'Kessom,' repeated Kira.

There was a muttered conversation and then the sound of orders being issued. Boots gritted over the paving and then the clip of hoofs as other horses came alongside. Kira was barely aware of them, of the mare's sweat and snort as she climbed, or of the wind's sigh in the Tiar Forests. She did not notice the daylight ebb, or the lands steepen either and it was the roaring that finally penetrated her senses. It was dark and an icy mist beaded her jacket.

The Guard brought their small procession to a stop, dismounted to confer, and then one of them came back to her. 'This part of the journey is dangerous, Lady. The river's high and the path is perilous even in daylight. There's been rain too. Guard Storsil and I will take you and the mare through first. Then we must leave you for a time and return for our horses. There's no threat to you on the northern side.'

He held out his hand and Kira realized he wanted her to dismount. She did so clumsily, and he fastened a length of rope around her waist. It reminded her of what Jonred had done when he had retrieved her from Ember Chasm.

Storsil took one end of the rope and led the way while the second Guard took the other end and followed. There was a black roaring below and, as she numbly recalled it was where Tierken's father had drowned, she understood their strange mode of travel. If Storsil slipped, he would let go of the rope, rather than drag her into the water with him, as would the Guard behind. They would drown but if Kira slipped, she would be held by them both.

It started to rain, increasing the path's slickness, and making it harder to see. Like most Tremen, Kira's night vision was acute from the seasons spent in the trees' muted light, but the Gaurds' was not and the terrible thought came to her that she might have murdered them as well as the Tremen volunteers.

11

The dirges had been sung in Tain, Terak, Kir and Illian, and now the only sound was the spit of burning flesh as the flames engulfed the last of the pyres. Tierken stood with bowed head, his men to either side completing the pyre's circle. Further out on the plain, the Tain burned the Shargh. Tierken would have left them to the marwings and wolves, seeing no reason to honor in death those who had no honor in life, but he was in Tain lands and Adris did as he saw fit.

It was Tierken's final night with the Tain King. On the morrow, he would turn north, leaving Adris's men to finish off the few Shargh who had eluded them. They had hunted the Shargh over flatlands, ridgelands and stonelands, under moonlight and starlight, through storms and days as clear as glass. The Weshargh Leader had been felled with his horse and, without him, his warriors had proved easy pickings. Of the Soushargh, there had been no sign.

Scurried back to their skin huts, Adris had said contemptuously. Tierken was less sure but alone, the Soushargh were too few to pose a threat. The Cashgar Leader had escaped, bearing the mark of Jonred's sword across his face, but most of his warriors fed the fires behind Tierken. His lip curled as he considered the Ashmiri. They had taken their animals east again, having *wisely* decided to herd not fight.

The flames sank low on the pyre and with a final bow, Tierken made his way back to camp. Adris strode out to meet him, bearing a cup of ale. 'Let us give thanks to Meros and Irid, to the strength of our men, and to a friendship regained between our peoples,' said Adris in toast.

'And to our last night together,' added Tierken, as they drained their cups. There was no need to talk of treaty and obligation, of loyalty and trust. They were as brothers, and that was enough.

The night was fine and the dawn gentle, and Tierken led his men north before the sun crested the horizon. He kept the pace steady although he yearned to gallop all the way to Sarnia. There was still danger, despite the plain seeming empty and it took only a single spear to lose a man or horse. Tierken refused to surrender either, especially by being careless.

He'd had no messages from Sarnia for a half moon, nor had expected any. Their pace and dispersal over the Sarsalin made it difficult for messengers to track them, and Tierken preferred they did not risk their lives in trying. The last news he had received was from Marin, which consisted of what Farid sent in a scroll, and what the gossips spoke of in Sarnia's streets.

Kira had yet to fully recover from saving Healer Tresen, but refused to leave the Haelen to rest, a selflessness that had earned her respect and affection in Sarnia, but Tierken would have preferred she was held in contempt, if the price were her well-being.

Both Farid and Marin reported Laryia continued to keep company with *Tremen Healer* Tresen. Perhaps the call of blood to blood ran in his family, thought Tierken acidly, as he considered Kira. Farid's first reports had made Tierken wonder whether Laryia felt sympathy for

Kira's clanmate rather than affection, but the messages since, both official and unofficial, suggested they courted.

Niria nursed Tresen in the Domain but Laryia never went to his rooms. She met with him only in the square, in full view of the servers. They sat closely but did not touch and the gossips agreed the Lady Laryia had never looked more beautiful, and that the cause of her joy was *Tremen Healer* Tresen.

Tierken grunted. Laryia had always been beautiful and it was not the supposed change in her looks that convinced him she was serious about Tresen. It was her caution. Laryia had long shrugged off rumors seeded by her time with Farid. *They can believe I share my bed with Rosham, for all I care,* she had scoffed. Well, she certainly cared now.

The journey was pleasant with dwinhir performing their dances overhead and young silverjacks breaking from the grasses at their approach. Only the rotting remains of horses and the occasional Shargh corpse marred their pleasure. Tierken and his men spat on the first in contempt at the Ashmiri's duplicity, and on the second in hatred.

The warmth had had its effect on the Silvercades too with the Breshlin Ford the deepest Tierken had seen. The rushing water came almost to Kalos's girth and Tierken forded first and secured a rope across to aid the smaller horses. He ordered camp to be set early too, despite his eagerness to reach Sarnia, knowing his men needed time without fighting or travel.

Their meal was unhurried and they sang that night, but there were no lay-links; the fighting had forced the herders far to the north or to the shelter of Sarnia's walls.

The Kirs sang of herding as usual, and the Kessomis of the mountains, but the Terak and Illians sang of the women they had left behind and, although Tierken had sang the songs countless times, he had never felt them as he did now.

They broke camp before dawn and were halfway to Ges Grove when the scouts reported a messenger. Tierken rode on ahead to meet him, enjoying the hard gallop as much as Kalos, and eager for news.

It was Ayled, who had been with the patrols stationed at the city's back. 'I've searched for you these past days, Feailner,' he said apologetically, as he delivered the message cylinder with a bow.

Tierken read quickly and his hand clenched on the paper. 'How many days, Ayled?'

'Four since I set out, Feailner.'

Tierken's jaw clenched. Kira had gone to Kessom at a time when water roared through Glass Gorge like the Silvercades' gales. What in Irid's name had possessed Farid to let her go? One slip was all it took. There was no way out of the torrent and no second chance.

'Take message to Anvorn to bring the men in,' ordered Tierken. 'I go to Sarnia.'

He wrenched Kalos around and rode hard till dusk, rested Kalos briefly then rode hard again, and it was dusk on the second day when he reached the Rehan. Kalos went with his head down and Tierken felt scarcely better. He briefly acknowledged the Tallien and the men he commanded there but did not stop.

A storm of chimes greeted him as he neared the wall and people lined the path to the Domain to cheer him and throw flowers. He waved to them and forced himself to smile. He had imagined his triumphant homecoming many times during the fighting, and always with pleasure, but now all he felt was anger.

Ryn was at the stables and they embraced. 'It's good to have you back, Feailner,' he said and eyed Kalos. 'You've worked the stallion hard.'

'His work isn't finished,' said Tierken. 'I'll need him on the morrow.'

'The next day, Feailner.'

Tierken grunted. 'The next day then, Horse Master.' He strode across the square to where Farid and Laryia waited and was less than halfway to them before Laryia sprinted to him and threw herself into his arms.

'Thank Irid you're safe,' she repeated over and over again, her face wet with tears. 'I love you so much.'

'And I you,' he said intensely, then released her and embraced Farid. 'It's good to see you, Keeper.'

'And *you*, my friend,' replied Farid with feeling.

'I'll join you shortly, Farid, but first I must speak with my sister.'

Farid bowed. 'I'll await you in the Meeting Hall.'

Laryia led the way to her rooms and settled at the table but Tierken prowled around the room.

'Kira went to Kessom without me or Farid knowing,' she said quietly.

Tierken swung back to her. 'The reports said she was ill. Why didn't you care for her?'

'There were too many wounded for either of us to rest. As soon as I could, I sent her back to the Domain. That's when she left.'

'Then what possessed Guard Leader Tharin to let her go?'

'He warned her of the state of the Gorge and advised her against the journey. You know that is all he can do.

When she refused his advice, he sent Guard with her.'

'So three drown instead of one! Have you message from Kessom?'

'No. They wouldn't risk travel.'

'So we don't know if *any* of them survived the Gorge?'

'No.'

'Why go to Kessom anyway?' he demanded, pacing again.

'I think Kira knew she needed the care of another Healer. The constant taking of pain—'

Tierken rounded on her furiously. 'I forbade her from doing that!'

Laryia thrust back her chair and stood. 'Kira's a Healer, Tierken! Without her skill, many who live now would be dead. Tresen would be dead!'

Laryia flushed and Tierken's eyes narrowed as he surveyed her. 'The reports say you court, that there's love between you.'

'The reports are true.'

'Is it love?'

'I know the difference between sunlight and shadow, Tierken.'

'The Tremen don't marry, Laryia. I won't have you as *his woman*.'

'Tresen understands what our customs demand. We wait only for your permission.'

'And if I withhold it?'

'You've no reason to, Tierken. You've recognized the Tremen as kin.'

'You realize that as Kira won't return south, Tresen must. After Kira, they say he's the best Healer and Tremen Leaders are chosen on Healer skill.'

'We've spoken of it,' said Laryia.

'You would go to Allogrenia with him?'

'Yes.'

Tierken rubbed the back of his neck. 'So, my choice is to lose you or to lose Kira.'

'You'll never lose me,' said Laryia, going to him and taking his hands. 'If Sarnia now welcomes Kasheron's seed, then Allogrenia must welcome Terak's.' Tierken said nothing, and Laryia smiled tremulously. 'I know this is hard for you, Tierken, especially after the terrible moons of fighting, but I'm asking for your blessing to marry the man I love, and with whom I want to spend the rest of my days, whatever those days might bring. Will you give it to me?'

Tierken contemplated her grimly. If Laryia married Tresen she would be far from him, the safety of Sarnia's walls and from the Guards' protection but the alternative was to deny his permission, hope her misery would pass and that, one day, she would love someone more suitable. No doubt there were many in Sarnia who hoped he would love someone *more suitable* too.

Laryia still waited and Tierken kissed her formally on each cheek. 'I love you, Laryia, and desire your happiness above all else. If you believe it lies with Tremen Healer Tresen, then I give you my permission and my blessing to wed him.'

Laryia's eyes widened and she threw her arms around his neck. Tierken felt wetness soak into his shirt again. 'Too much weeping,' he said.

'They're tears of joy,' she choked.

'I go to the Meeting Hall now. There's much I need to discuss with Farid. On the morrow, I'll return to the Rehan to speak with the Lord Caledon and the men there. The next day I go to Kessom. Depending on what I find there, it could be another moon before I return. That should give you time to make your marriage preparations. How does Tremen Healer Tresen?'

'He grows stronger but cannot yet walk.'

'When would you wed then?'

'At the beginning of summer.'

It would be a good time for two weddings, thought Tierken. Tresen's willingness to marry proved that Tremen traditions were no real impediment to marriage and now the fighting was finished, he had time to build Kira's trust, assuming his bride-to-be had survived Glass Gorge.

12

Tierken timed his journey to Kessom to ensure he passed through Glass Gorge in daylight. He wanted to reduce the dangers to him and Kalos, but he also wanted to search for signs of Kira and the Guard too. Silver Falls' thunder was audible from the Frost Glades and by the time he neared the gorge, spume fell like rain. Kalos snorted and Tierken dismounted. The gorge was a surge of boiling water, full of mud and broken branches, and he scanned the path.

There were hoof prints, but it was impossible to tell how many horses had passed through, and there were boot prints too, but only large ones. The prints were deep which told him the path had been wet. Kira and the Guard had left Sarnia a little after midday and would have reached here at night. His skin crawled. Darkness and a slick path; it was hard to imagine a deadlier combination.

He murmured to Kalos soothingly as he edged along the path and tried not to look down at the torrent. Even if all three of them had fallen, there would be no trace, but the prints suggested at least one Guard had survived the trek, an understanding that brought him no comfort at all.

Tierken forced himself not to hurry, not wanting to risk ending his days in the water, and it seemed an age before the path broadened and he could mount again. He continued as fast as he dared, but it was well dark before he reached Kessom and, for once, Robrin was nowhere to be found.

There was no sign of Kira's mare either and his guts clenched. Kessom had four other stables and Robrin oversaw them all but it did nothing to ease his tension. He swiftly rubbed Kalos down then sprinted up the path to Eris's house, beat on the door, paused, and beat again. It seemed an age before Eris opened it.

'Is Kira here?' he demanded.

'Yes. Kira and the Guard arrived safely.'

He briefly shut his eyes. 'Thank Irid! She's in Laryia's room?' he demanded, snatching up a lamp.

Eris's bony hand closed over his arm. 'Let her be,' she ordered. 'She sleeps so light you'll wake her, if you haven't already. There's time enough on the morrow.'

Tierken followed Eris to the cooking place and threw himself into a chair. 'Tell me how she is,' he said.

'Kira was exhausted when she arrived, but that was a moon third ago,' said Eris. 'Since then she's slept and eaten, and gathered, worked herbs into salves and pastes, and sat with me.'

Eris poured him cotzee and loaded cheese and maizen bread onto a plate, but Tierken barely noticed. 'But is she well?'

'Exhaustion and a constant dealing with death will make anyone ill, and Kira is no exception, but she will heal. All she needs is time to see what is good and beautiful in the world again.'

'I don't know how long I can stay; there's much to be done in Sarnia. Has Kira spoken of me?'

'No.'

'Of the Lord Caledon then?'

'No,' said Eris, and smiled at Tierken's expression. 'Don't fret, Tierken. When you first brought Kira here, I saw her love for you and it's no different now. But you must give her time.'

112

Tierken had not expected to sleep but the fighting had left him with a deep weariness and the sun was well up before he woke and hurried to the cooking place. Only Eris was there, busy at her grinding. 'Kira still sleeps?' he demanded.

'She sleeps less than you,' said Eris. 'She gathers for me and will be back soon. Sit and have your breakfast.' Tierken fidgeted around the cooking place, straining for sounds of her return.

'Sit,' ordered Eris.

Tierken sat. His neck crawled and he distracted himself by watching steam from the maizen mash, pattern the air, and then the outer door opened and closed and footsteps sounded and she was there. Her hair was longer and fairer than he recalled, and it fell over her face as she bent to extricate herself from the herbal sling.

He had stood, though he had no recollection of doing so, and as she straightened, her face filled with wonder. Then she was in his arms, the feel of her strange and familiar, simultaneously making him whole and conscious of loss. She was skin and bones, her eyes the dark green he had only ever seen at her most distressed. 'I want you now, before this dream finishes, before I wake,' she whispered.

'It's no dream, I'm here with you, in Eris's house, in Kessom.'

'I don't believe you.'

'Ah, that proves it's not a dream,' said Tierken, forcing his voice to lightness. 'In a dream I'm sure you'd believe me, but in waking life you never did.'

'Not *never*!'

'Not often then,' he corrected, maintaining his bantering tone despite his shock at her gauntness.

Eris had disappeared, so Tierken spooned out the mash while Kira collected the herbs spilled from her sling. She stared at him and he watched her, so neither made a good job of their task.

Kira ate little but Tierken stopped himself from scolding her. 'You wear Kasheron's ring,' she said as they ate.

'The ring of both our peoples.'

Her eyes came to his, and while their darkness masked their usual reassuring softening, love shone in her face. 'Why did you accept the kin-link, Tierken?'

He half shrugged. 'The Lord Caledon and Farid added more knowing to what you told me,' he said briefly, not wanting to revisit old quarrels.

'Is the fighting finished?'

'Yes. The Shargh won't be turning their murderous eyes north *or* south again. Your people are safe.'

Kira dropped her head and there was a long silence. 'No more wounds, no more dying, no more death,' she muttered, and then her dark eyes fastened on his. 'You've spoken with Laryia about Tresen?'

'Yes.'

'And?'

The sunshine that shafted in through the open shutters lit the angular planes of her face and her fine hands at rest on the table looked fragile now, as she did. By Irid, he wanted her safe in Sarnia as his wife, away from the life-destroying effects of Healing.

He lay his hand over hers. 'I've given them my blessing. Healer Tresen is willing to marry in the Terak way, so we—' Kira's hand clenched under his and Tierken stopped. There would be time enough later to raise the topic of *their* marriage. He smiled and smoothed the hair from her face. 'I have meetings I must attend to today, but on the morrow, I'd like to take you into the mountains, to the Kristlin and the Foaling Fields, and to all the beautiful places I roamed in my growing,' he said. 'Would you like that?'

Kira smiled but her eyes did not change. 'Yes,' she said. 'I would.'

They set off early the next day, Tierken shouldering a heavy pack of food and Kira a pack with warm clothing, a sleeping-sheet and a Healer's kit. The first part of the journey was through the lands where she had gathered but as they gradually climbed higher, the mountains soared in front of them and Kessom dropped away behind.

The alwaysgreen groves thickened and mountain streams tinkled over stones, crystal clear and shockingly cold. Tierken kept the pace easy with lots of rest breaks where they perched on boulders and ate maizen bread and dried fruit. He named the snowy birds that pecked insects from the stones, and showed her the burrows of mead-mice, mountain hares and whitejacks. Smaller paths ran off here and there, mossy from small use, and dwinhirs swooped overhead. 'Still dancing,' he said, with a smile.

Kira said little, still struggling with the bleakness that had prompted her flight from Sarnia. It sat like a sheet of ice between her and everything else, making it hard to think clearly and draining pleasure from the things she loved. Eris said time and rest would send cure and her Healer-self knew it was true and in the meantime, all that mattered was Tierken was with her.

Kira watched him as they walked. He was leaner and more muscled, his movements more abrupt, and he scanned continuously, but when he smiled at her, he was the same; his love a beam of sunlight that made her heart sing.

They took their midday meal high above Kessom. Eris's house was hidden by alwaysgreens but Tierken pointed out Thalli's house, the Keshall and the southern stables. 'Have you named your mare yet?' he asked.

'No.'

'The mare's been left nameless far too long,' he chided. 'We can think of names as we walk. I'll start by nominating *Beautiful*, after you.'

'Your men name their horses after the weather or the mountains,' said Kira, bleakness blunting her pleasure in his compliment.

'Yes, but it's not necessary. Laryia called her mare Chime and I called Kalos after an old Kessomi word for strength. Is there something in Allogrenia you might name her for?'

'There's the mira kiraon, but I can hardly name her after myself. The other owls are the hanawey and frostking. Then there are springleslips and tippets and honeysprites—which are birds, or lissium, which is a plant with a sweet white flower. There are moon moths and silver moths and flutterwings . . .' Tears slid down her face, and Kira wiped them away.

She had rarely wept in Allogrenia or in the terrible times since, and was dismayed that she had wept most days since being in Kessom. Eris said it was exhaustion and would pass. Tierken drew her into his arms, but Kira felt foolish and weak, like a child with no control over their emotions.

It was early evening when Tierken led her off the track and through a stand of slender, white-trunked trees

116

to a single-roomed building. It was shingle-roofed and its timber walls silvered with age. A *shelter-hut*, Tierken called it, and said similar huts were scattered through the Silvercades to aid the traveler. The single window was shuttered, making it dark and chill inside, but Tierken soon had a fire burning, nuts roasting, and water heating for cotzee.

The smell of roasting nuts reminded Kira of the Bough, of Miken's longhouse, of her early days with Tierken's patrol, and some of her dull-headedness dissipated. She became aware of the firelight's slide over Tierken's hair and reached out to touch it. She had forgotten how soft it was, and he turned his head and smiled. It was Kandor's smile but also his own.

'I want you,' she whispered.

Tierken lifted the pan of nuts from the fire and turned to her. 'We'll do things properly this time, Kira, like Laryia and Tresen have.'

Kira tried to recall how Laryia and Tresen behaved but that time was lost in a fog of death and dying. All she remembered was Laryia sitting beside Tresen's pallet in the Haelen and once Tresen had been moved to the Domain, Laryia reporting how he fared.

Kira half shook her head. All she knew was she needed Tierken's love. She reached for him again but he caught her hands in his. 'Laryia and Tresen have had the benefit of more time together than we have,' he said. 'Tresen loves Laryia and shows his love by accepting the Terak custom of marriage. Laryia might go to your lands but whether she goes or stays in Sarnia, she can only receive the respect owed to her, as Tresen's wife not *his woman*.

'There's been no time for you to come to trust I would never give you cause to regret marrying me. We have that time now, Kira, and I have my mother's pledge bracelet with me. I've asked you to marry me twice before but I won't ask you a third time this night, for I know it's too soon for you, but I will ask you before we return to Sarnia. Until then, we'll court as my sister and your clanmate do.'

Kira understood little of what he had said other than he was to deny her his Shelter, and she jerked her hands from his. 'You don't want me,' she said brokenly.

'I want you more than anything in the world but as my wife. Until we're pledged, I want us to enjoy sharing things we need to know to be happy in our coming marriage.'

Abruptly anger did what Laryia, Farid and Eris's kindness had failed to. It smashed the dullness that enclosed her and what she saw, with the sparkling clarity of the mountain streams, was the choice Tierken offered. To have his love, the sweet feel of his skin next to hers and the ecstasy of his Shelter, she must wear metal and promise to stay in Sarnia forever. That was the trade he offered, no matter how nicely he dressed it up. If there was to be love, it was to be on his terms.

Tierken handed her a bowl of nuts and a cup of cotzee and Kira nodded her thanks, and when she had finished, she pulled her sleeping-sheet from her pack and lay down next to the fire. 'The bed's softer,' said Tierken, gesturing to the raised wooden platform behind them, a grass mattress already in place.

Kira said nothing. She was very tired, and despite her boiling thoughts, it was only a short time before she slept.

13

Kira woke to stiff, sore muscles and it was late morning before they eased. She had exercised little in Sarnia, even before the fighting had confined her to the Haelen, while in Allogrenia, she had roamed beyond the Third Eight and set her sleeping-sling in ashaels or terrawoods.

Living in Sarnia meant only journeying within the walls and she was even loath to do that, for she was never alone. The Guard meant she must consider her every action and word, even down to not cursing if she stubbed her toe. And if she somehow managed to forget their presence, eyes slid sideways from those she passed or peered at her from behind shutters.

It was scarcely better in Kessom, with Storsil and the other Guard, *Farsrin*, insisting on accompanying her whenever she gathered. And even here, where sunny meads stretched away, dotted with white and yellow flowers, Tierken confined her with threats of metal and marriage.

As they walked, he spoke of the Foaling Fields they would reach later that day, of how the blood of the stallion Ralis, brought from beyond the Oskinas in seasons long past, ran truest in the horses there, and of how horses of his line were sought after in all the northern, western and eastern lands. The bloodline was never traded from his family and Kalos, Chime and Kira's own mare were all of that line.

His words fed Kira's anger for Tierken had obviously gifted her the mare on the expectation she would join *his* family through marriage and so, Kira's ownership of the mare was actually dependent on Tierken's ownership of *her*. There seemed little point in naming the mare then, for Kira had no intention of becoming Tierken's *property*.

As the day wore on, her anger enlarged to include Tresen, for his speedy acquiescence to Terak ways had strengthened Tierken's belief that Kira's objections to marriage were unreasonable and could be overcome.

The constant churn of thoughts robbed her of enjoyment in their travel and she bit her lip as she struggled to impose order on her weary brain. Perhaps her objections *were* unreasonable. Perhaps the whole notion of marriage had got tangled up with everything else she'd had to fight Tierken for: recognition of the kin-link and aid for the Tremen; the creation of the Haelen and her right to gather, heal and take pain; and the freedom to come and go unhampered by Guard and without begging his permission.

She *had* offered to bond with him which meant staying in Sarnia and accommodating nearly every other Terak custom, but it was not enough for him and now he punished her by withholding himself.

They reached the second shelter-hut mid afternoon and Tierken deposited the pack inside before he took Kira's hand and led her to where the trees gave way to a solid wall of boulders. He slipped between them and Kira gasped as she saw the land fall away in a dizzying drop. Far away on the valley floor, made tiny by distance, were horses.

'The smaller dark ones you can see are the first of this season's foals. All silver horses are born dark and lighten over their first three seasons. Your mare's reached the color she'll stay. Have you thought of a name for her yet?'

'No.'

'I still favor Beautiful,' said Tierken with a smile, as his fingers tilted her face to his.

Kira stepped back. 'We're not allowed to kiss, remember.'

'I never said that. I just want us to take things more slowly, to spend more time coming to know each other, so that you learn to trust—'

'You didn't ask me what I wanted!'

'I thought you loved me,' he said.

'I do! But you won't have me! You want this other thing, where I'm with you but not with you!' Kira struggled to control her temper and failed, her fury fed by the long moons of longing and fear for him. 'You think that by holding yourself apart, I'll marry you, but you're wrong! I won't marry you *or* Caledon *or* any other man! The Tremen don't marry!'

Tierken's face was suddenly very cold. 'Tresen has pledged to marry Laryia. Are telling me he's lied to my sister *and* to me?'

'He's only doing it to please her!'

'And you're not willing to please me?'

Kira pushed a shaking hand through her hair. 'I offered to trade away Allogrenia *to please you*, to never see Miken and Tenerini and Kest again *to please you*, but I can't change into a Terak *to please you*! I'll always be a Tremen Healer.'

'Without marriage you won't be *a Tremen Healer*, you'll be akin to a Caru woman!'

'I don't care what's said about me on the streets of Sarnia,' cried Kira. 'I don't even care if Rosham spits at me again. All I care is that you give me your love!'

Tierken's hand flashed to his sword. 'Rosham spat at you?'

'It doesn't matter,' said Kira, regretting her slip. 'As long as you're with me, nothing matters!'

'You don't understand *anything* about Sarnia if you believe that!' he said, already striding back towards the hut. 'I regret that our sightseeing of the Silvercades must be cut short. I'm returning to Sarnia. You will remain in Kessom until the end of spring when you will be collected for Laryia's wedding.'

He walked so fast Kira had to jog to keep up. 'I don't care about Rosham, Tierken. It's not important.'

Tierken reclaimed his pack from the hut and slammed the door shut. 'Tremen ways aren't Terak ways, as you've pointed out to me on *many* occasions, and if it's acceptable for the Tremen to insult their leader, I'm glad they're not!'

He strode off and Kira hurried along behind. 'The insult was aimed at me, Tierken. For my sake, let it be,' she begged.

'This started before your time and I'm going back to end it.'

'But I want you here with me!'

He stopped and swung back to her. 'If that were really true, Kira, you would marry me.'

Kira had to use all her strength just to keep Tierken in sight as he strode along, and by the time they reached the next shelter-hut, she was so weary she simply crawled into her sleeping-sheet. Tierken built the fire, then heated water and roasted nuts. 'Don't go to sleep before you eat,' he warned, but Kira already drifted and then she was in the nightmare of Kandor's death.

She woke with a scream, as she always did and lay panting in fright, and then Tierken was suddenly beside her, his comforting hand on her arm. 'Tell me what you dream,' he said gently.

'No!' she said, pulling the sleeping-sheet close.

'I want to share these things with you, for you to trust me.'

She turned on him furiously. 'How can I trust you when every time I don't bow to your will, you take back your love? When I have to pretend to be other than I am to gain your approval? When you say you want me, but walk away when I displease you? Caledon was right when he said you would never accept me!'

Tierken's face hardened. 'You seem to believe the Lord Caledon is immune from error *and* from the desire to arrange things to his own liking.'

'Where is he now?' she demanded.

'Why do you ask?'

'Because he helped save Allogrenia, *and* Tresen, and he helped me in the Azurcades. I want to see him again, to speak with him, to thank him. Has he gone back to Talliel?'

'He's in Maraschin but will be a guest at Laryia's wedding. Then I presume he'll return to Talliel, for there's nothing to keep him here.'

Kira stared at the fire as she thought of the thumbelin's sweet music and of his Shelter on Shardos. 'I'll miss him,' she said, in a small voice.

The crack of burning wood filled the silence and then she felt Tierken's fingers on her face and closed her eyes as he caressed her cheek and slowly turned her face to his. His lips were soft and his kisses gentle, and she clung to him, overwhelmed by her need for his Shelter, but then he pulled back. 'Is the Tremen Feailner still willing to bond with the Terak Feailner?'

She stared at him in confusion. 'I'm willing,' she said uncertainly.

'Then explain to me how it is done.'

'The . . . the couple who are to bond come before the Tremen Leader at Turning—that's a celebration to mark spring turning to summer. There's a time during the celebration—usually near the end—when those who are to bond step forward and recite their pledge.'

'That's all? There's no exchange of rings or bracelets and nothing's recorded?'

'No. The Clanleaders and others present take the news back to their longhouses and it's soon known who's bonded.'

'So, as you're the Tremen Leader and can't come before yourself, would it be sufficient for us to simply recite this bonding pledge now? Or must we have witnesses? Laryia and Tresen are to wed at the start of summer but I want to keep this separate.'

'I don't think we need witnesses,' said Kira, unable to recall any precedent.

'Then let us delay no longer.'

Kira felt dizzy at the pace things unfolded. On the rare occasions she had imagined bonding, it had not been dressed in travel-stained clothing with her hair in her eyes, but nor had her musings prepared her for the power of her feelings for this man.

'If you speak first, I can follow your words, *unless* the man must speak first,' said Tierken.

'I don't think it matters,' said Kira, and took a deep breath. 'I, Kiraon of Kashclan, daughter of Maxen, daughter of Fasarini, sister of Merek, sister of Lern, sister of Kandor, speak now at Turn—*speak now*, that I choose

Tierken of the Terak Kirillian as bondmate and Shelter, until leaf-fall and branch-fall shall end all my days.'

Kira's throat tightened but she smiled at Tierken through her tears as he started his pledge. 'I, Tierken of the Terak Kirillian, son of Merench, son of Lyess, brother of Laryia, speak now, that I choose Kiraon of Kashclan as bondmate and Shelter, until leaf-fall and branch-fall shall end all my days.'

Kira kissed Tierken formally on each cheek. 'Welcome to Kashclan,' she said tremulously.

'I didn't realize Kashclan came with the pledge,' he said, bending to toss more wood on the fire. 'It's late and we have a long journey on the morrow to Kessom. It's best you get some sleep, Kira.'

'You're still going back to Sarnia?' she asked in bewilderment.

'Of course,' said Tierken. 'Nothing's changed.'

14

The last of the ghastly parade of Shargh survivors did not straggle back to the Grounds until after the new moon. They bore sword slashes and arrow wounds, crushed bones from the stamp of the massive Northern horses and broken bones from falls from the Ashmiri ones. All were weak from lack of food and some had coughs that gurgled like streams.

They told wild tales of the Northerners calling up magic to spring from trees, to raise rivers into flood, and to go without food and sleep for days on end. And they told of the Ashmiri's betrayal. Few blamed Arkendrin outright *or* the Sky Chiefs, but there were bitter words whispered within sorcha walls and wailing as many who survived the long trek back, sickened and died.

Irdodun was one of the few to escape unscathed, and his join-wife and daughters tended Arkendrin. His eye socket had filled with pus and, as he burned with fever, his ravings were audible from the top sorcha. Palansa kept Ersalan inside, fearful of the drift of ill vapors from the lower sorcha. She hoped the wound would claim Arkendrin's life, but the Sky Chiefs had shown they had no intention of calling Arkendrin home yet.

Tarkenda said he still had a part to play in the Last Telling but Palansa dreaded what it might be and she contemplated all he had done as she paced around her Sorcha. His hunting of the gold-eyed Healer had already brought much of the Telling into being and now the deaths of their warriors meant nothing prevented the Northerners coming to kill everyone on the Grounds.

The possibility so terrified Palansa that she scooped up Ersalan from the sleep-sling and held him close. Tarkenda believed the Telling was as set as the Thanawah was within its banks, but Palansa hoped the Sky Chiefs' had gifted it as a warning too, and in doing so, given the Shargh the chance to avoid it.

She paused and her mind raced and then she went to where Ormadon and Erlken sat outside the door. 'Send Irason to me,' she said.

They looked at her in surprise but Erlken rose to do her bidding. Palansa wandered around the sorcha while she waited, returning Ersalan's smiles despite her seething thoughts and eventually a gravelly voice sounded at the door-flap and Palansa bade Irason to enter.

He palmed to Ersalan, then to her, but he was so bent he was scarcely taller when he straightened. 'How might I serve the Chief and the Chief-mother?' he asked.

Irason served Arkendrin, not Ersalan or her, but the old Shargh had something she needed. 'You can teach me the Northern tongue,' she said, 'and you can start now.'

Tresen sat with Laryia next to the Owl Fountain. The woodrights had crafted him a chair that allowed him to be carried to and from his room and Laryia had made it soft with cushions and snug with covers. The square trapped the spring sunshine and for once he was overly warm. He flicked off the cover and grimaced at the sight of his wasted legs.

While most things had been a blur since his wounding, his first glimpse of Laryia remained graven in his mind and now, beyond all hope, the Northern Feailner had granted them permission to marry. Given Tresen's dealings with

Laryia's brother, he had expected a long and bitter struggle to secure the Northern Feailner's consent and he suspected he could thank the Feailner's love for Kira for his speedy agreement.

Even so, the Feailner might have applied a different rule to his own behavior, as the powerful often did, and Tresen acknowledged the Feailner's honesty in not doing so. Yet he still found it hard to warm to the man and he wondered how Laryia had turned out so differently.

Laryia's beauty had always enthralled him but it was her sweetness and strength that had won his heart. She spoke to him as if he were already recovered and the only impediment to them going to the Southern Forests was the need for him to learn to ride. Nor would Laryia countenance any difficulty in settling into life there. Having been raised in Kessom, she was well used to trees, she assured him, and Kira had told her much about the Tremen manner of living.

When pain wracked him and he trembled with weakness, Tresen despaired of ever being well again and he wondered why Laryia had chosen him when she could have had any *hale* man in Sarnia or in the rest of the Terak lands, for that matter. Then her warm hand would close over his and his doubts vanish.

As they sat enjoying the spring sun, they spoke of the Kashclan longhouse again, for Laryia was keen to know of the kin who would soon be hers, and Tresen was just describing some of Brem's foibles when they heard bells.

'Tierken's back,' said Laryia in surprise. 'That's strange, he's only been gone a few days. I hope the news isn't ill.'

They waited in silence, both fearing that Kira *had* drowned in Glass Gorge but neither willing to say it. The

128

Domain gate swung open and Kalos cantered through, Tierken heading to the stables first to hand the stallion to Ryn, before striding towards them. 'I fear the news *is* ill,' whispered Laryia, her gaze on Tierken's face.

'Tremen Healer Tresen,' said Tierken, with a nod. 'I trust your recovery continues?'

'It does. I thank you, Feailner,' said Tresen.

'Is Kira safe?' asked Laryia.

'She's in Kessom where she will remain for the time being,' said Tierken, his attention still on Tresen. 'I regret I must rob you of your company for a short while, Tremen Healer. I must speak with my sister about matters that occurred during my absence. We shouldn't be long.'

He strode off and with final glance at Tresen, Laryia hurried after him to the Meeting Hall, holding her silence until they were inside. 'Why have you returned so quickly?' she asked. 'Is it well between you and Kira?'

'We've bonded.'

'Oh, Tierken!' She threw her arms around him. 'I'm so happy for you.'

'You shouldn't be,' he said, disengaging himself. 'Kira's status remains scarcely higher than a Caru woman's.'

'All isn't well, is it?'

'I didn't request your company to discuss Kira but to discover why you neglected to tell me Rosham spat at her.'

Laryia's eyes widened. 'I didn't know he had,' she breathed. 'Of course, Rosham was furious you recognized the kin-link, but that was to be expected.'

'What did he say?'

'I'll not repeat his exact words, but I threatened him with expulsion, and he apologized—after a fashion.'

'Tell me what he said!'

'He said Kira was like a Caru woman who had used her body to make you forget your obligations and duties,' said Laryia reluctantly.

'He's fortunate I'm only going to expel him,' gritted Tierken.

'I ask that you don't.'

'You think his insults are acceptable?' he demanded.

'Of course not! But if you expel him, he'll garner sympathy and use it against you *and* Kira and any Tremen who settle here. There's a better punishment.'

'Which is?'

'Make him irrelevant, Tierken.'

Tierken's eyes narrowed. 'What mean you?'

'By-pass him and the rest of the Marken. Speak directly with the trader leaders. With the Wastes to be opened up, the traders will have great demand for their goods. Involve them in the procurement of building supplies too.'

'I want that man out of Sarnia!'

'Yes, I do too, but you need to consider Farid. He is absolutely loyal to you and to the Domain, but Rosham is his father. It would shame him to have Rosham expelled.'

'Yet *you* threatened him with expulsion.'

'Yes, and it would have given me a great deal of pleasure to do so but, for Kira's sake, the Tremen *must* gain the city's acceptance and the trader leaders are the key to that, not Rosham and his ilk.'

Tierken nodded abruptly. 'But if Rosham *ever* shows even the *slightest* disrespect to Kira or to other Tremen, he'll never pass the gate again. You can let Farid know.'

'I will, but there's something I want to show you, Tierken. Come.' Tierken looked at her questioningly but followed her along the balcony. She did not go to her rooms, as he expected, but to Kira's.

'You recall asking me to remove metal from Kira's rooms when she first arrived, and how bare they were?' Tierken nodded, and Laryia smiled. 'Well, they're not bare anymore,' she said, and gestured to the shelves. They were crowded with beautifully carved stone and wooden ornaments. 'When Kira converted the old stables into a Haelen, *before* the fighting came North, Sarnians began to seek her healing. Just a few at first, but word of her skill soon spread. They left trade in return, of course, which Kira wanted nothing to do with and passed on to me and Farid, but they left her gifts as well.'

Laryia smiled. 'Gifts are a very particular way of showing appreciation, Tierken. At first they left silver bracelets and bowls and candle-holders but as the wounded patrolmen arrived *and* then Protectors, they left only wooden or stone gifts. They obviously learned from their patrolman husbands, sons and brothers, of the Tremen's dislike of metal and *respected* the Tremen's feelings.

'There were so many wounded that we shifted those who were recovering to their homes and visited them there or sent helpers to change dressings. The wounded Protectors were billeted with their friends.' She paused. 'There is much in Sarnia that already undermines Rosham's antagonism, Tierken, and those whose husbands, sons and brothers live only because of Kira, don't forget to whom they owe their lives.' There was a short silence. 'So,' said Laryia carefully. 'Has Kira recovered?'

'No, but Eris assures me she will.'

'And so you've bonded.'

'For what it's worth,' said Tierken, wandering around the room. 'It was that or nothing.'

'Tresen says that bonding is very serious,' said Laryia. Tierken said nothing and she tried again. 'Tresen also says that Kira's refusal to marry might be due to her father. Apparently he was a cold and domineering man.'

'And Healer Tresen suggests I'm the same?'

'Of course not! He suggests Kira is frightened of being confined like her father confined her.'

'Is that how Tresen sees marriage? Like a cage?'

Laryia's eyes flashed. 'If I had any doubts about Tresen's love for me, or mine for him, I wouldn't marry him, Tierken.'

'And if I had any doubts about *my* love for Kira, I wouldn't have asked her to marry me *twice*,' he retorted. 'It seems you've been more fortunate in your choice of *Tremen* than I have.'

Laryia sighed. 'It's obvious to everyone that Kira loves you, and given she's bonded with you, she clearly wants to be with you. I think she just needs more time.'

Tierken shrugged and took his leave but as he made his way back along the balcony, he realized Laryia was right. Everything that had happened in Kessom pointed to Kira wanting him as did their time together *before* Kessom. Even after their worst arguments, her want of him had been clear. His steps slowed. His strategy in dealing with her had been completely wrong. He had not defeated the Shargh by fighting the way *they* wanted, and he would not defeat Kira by giving her what *she* wanted.

His lips settled into a hard line. He had been right to leave Kira in Kessom, *without him*, until the end of spring but it was not going to be easy for either of them when she returned to Sarnia *if* he were to win.

The last full moon of spring had passed before Tresen took his first faltering steps. He was appalled by his weakness but Laryia was delighted to see him walk and her encouragement gladdened him. He still slept much of the day and Laryia spent the time helping Arlen in the Haelen. It was almost as busy as it had been during the fighting. Aching backs, children's coughs, men with sprains and breaks, and women whose babes either refused to suckle, or suckled too much and then whooped the milk back up.

The Marken and their families kept away but they were the exception. It seemed as if Sarnia made up for having been denied healing for uncounted seasons. Many of those who visited asked after the Lady Kira and expressed hopes for her quick return to health. Her exhaustion in their service, and recovery in Kessom, seemed to be widely known.

Laryia was also occupied with wedding preparations. The next Mid-market fell too late to trade for gowns, so she took those traded at the last Mid-market to the Kir metal-workers whose skills allowed them to draw metals out to thread-like thinness. Laryia had them fashion intricate patterns of silver into the neck and cuffs of her gown, and make a circlet set with white and blue stones for her hair.

She also had Kira's green gown similarly ornamented with gold, and a gold circlet with green stones made. Kira had pledged never to wear metal again after the last banquet, but it could not be helped. The Marriage Walk was led by the Feailner and his Consort, and Kira must be properly attired.

Laryia thought about Kira often, but no messages arrived from Eris to tell her how she fared. Eris was uncommunicative by nature, especially if her words must be directed towards the *stone city* and so Laryia's only information came from the men who brought herbs from

Kessom, and all they reported was that the Lady Kira had been seen out gathering.

They made no mention of her bonding to the Feailner and nor did Niria, who had a keen ear for what was said in Sarnia. Farid did not speak of it either which, given his closeness to Tierken, suggested he did not know.

Tierken's secrecy made Laryia uneasy as did the fact he seemed angry about the bonding rather than glad, but she held her silence. It was for Tierken to announce his changed status to Sarnia, not her. In any case, leading the Marriage Walk with Kira beside him, resplendent in the green and gold gown, and crowned with the gold circlet, would be announcement enough.

15

Tierken went to the Rehan Valley each day before dawn and did not return until after moonrise. Houses needed to be rebuilt and those who dwelled there needed to feel safe again. Tierken enjoyed working with his men, and with those who made the Rehan their home, but he also enjoyed the exhaustion that gifted him sleep each night. He had slept poorly since his return from the fighting and even the slightest sound woke him, and he found himself on his feet, sword drawn, ready for battle.

Tierken also met with the trader leaders to plan the development of the Wastes or *Kasheron's Quarter* as he tried to call it. Laryia's suggestion, that he deal more directly with the trader leaders, had born fruit, strengthening his feailnership while simultaneously sidelining the Marken. And despite the occasional allusion to the *uncertain status* of the Tremen Leader, which he grimly ignored, Tierken was gratified by how much goodwill Kira's selfless healing had generated.

The positive sentiments of the trader leaders might have made Tierken proud had he not been forced to witness Laryia's wedding preparations. And knowing that Tresen was willing to do what Kira refused to, galled him.

Kira's longing for her bondmate was temporarily displaced by fear for Eris, who had fallen ill soon after Tierken's departure. She burned with fever and a pain wracked her bones that she refused to let Kira take. Eris also refused to send message of her illness to Sarnia, not wanting to upset Laryia or disrupt her wedding preparations.

Kira ministered to her through the long nights but Thalli helped during the day and Jafiel came too. He was close to twelve seasons, leggy and awkward and with a dry sense of humor that reminded Kira of Kandor. He made her laugh, and for the first time since Kandor's death, she found joy as well as sorrow in her memories of him.

As the days passed and the Silvercades' mantle of snow retreated, Kira roamed further and further afield. She came to know the high meads and to delight in the small valleys with their clear icy streams. The crisp air sharpened the alwaysgreen's spice and stirred a longing for Allogrenia but it sated it too. Kessom was not Allogrenia, but its beauty was no less.

On one ramble, high above Kessom, she came upon a dwinhir nest with three eggs, and returned often to watch the mated pair care for them. She wished Tierken was there to share her pleasure as the eggs hatched into clumsy chicks, in fact, she just wished Tierken were with her even if they never left Kessom.

In Allogrenia, newly bonded couples were left undisturbed for several moons to enjoy each other's company, but she made light of their separation to Eris. *Tierken was a Feailner and Feailners were less free than other men to follow their personal wishes*, she said. It was something Kira had learned too when she became the Tremen Feailner. She had told Eris of their bonding but Eris slept a lot now and when she *was* awake, she mostly wanted to know of her granddaughter's intended husband, and of Allogrenia, where Laryia would live.

'Allogrenia's more like Kessom than Sarnia,' said Kira, as they sat together in the cooking place, 'but I fear

Laryia will miss the Silvercades, and I know she'll miss all the pretty things at Mid-market. Allogrenia has no traders.'

'If Terak go there, traders will follow and it will be better for Laryia if it's so. You already know how hard it is to live amongst strangers.'

'The Tremen will welcome Laryia,' said Kira defensively.

'Will they? A Terak *Kutan*?'

'Laryia's a Healer,' said Kira. 'And she'll go to Allogrenia as the bondmate of the Tremen's best Healer.'

'Second best,' corrected Eris with a smile.

The illness had left Eris frail but her eyes had lost none of their shrewdness. 'I wonder whether *you* have thought through the implications of *your* bonding, of how much you have given up,' she said.

Kira forced a smile. 'I've known for a long time that to have Tierken means not to have Allogrenia. 'I can't be here in the North with my bondmate *and* there in south with my clanmates, but I need to go back one last time, Eris. When I left, I didn't think I would live to cross the Dendora, let alone return. I was running, too terrified to even look back. I've never been to the alwaysgreens where my family is buried, never stood beneath their boughs, never listened to my family's voices in the whisper of their leaves. I need do that.'

Kira's yearning for Tierken grew and as the end of spring approached, she fidgeted about the cooking place or spent her time at the stables, scanning the track for horses. As soon as Tierken arrived, she planned to take him on a quick visit to the dwinhir nest. The chicks were half fluff and half feathers now and she knew Tierken would enjoy seeing them as much as she did.

But when horses finally appeared on the track from Sarnia, they bore only Guard Leader Tharin, Guard Second Daril, and a young female server who carried clothes, and ribbons to dress Kira's hair.

'The Feailner orders that we leave late this night, so that we reach Sarnia at midday on the morrow. He reminds you that celebrations for his sister's wedding have commenced,' intoned Tharin. 'He sends attire appropriate for the occasion and looks forward to welcoming you home.'

Tharin's face was emotionless but Kira fought back tears. She had assumed her bondmate would come, not send Guard, and his orders meant she had no time to properly farewell Thalli and Jafiel. To add to Kira's upset, the server insisted on dressing Kira's hair there and then.

Kira had to still her churning emotions while the server laboriously braided her hair and wove in the silver and black ribbons. The clothes were black, ornamented with silver, like those she had seen her bondmate wear. There was a high-collared jacket split at the back for riding, black trousers, and black knee-high boots also embellished with silver. The colors of the Domain, Kira realized apprehensively, which she was now part of through her bonding.

She changed into them and came back to the cooking place. 'You look every part a queen,' said Eris.

'I feel every part a traitor to Kasheron, wearing this metal,' muttered Kira.

'The Tremen and Terak are one now,' Eris reminded her.

'Metal's still prasach.'

Eris smiled and continued her grinding, but Kira's throat tightened as she watched the elderly Healer. She was going to miss her and the comforting familiarity of her house. The fire flickered low and the air was sweet with drying herbs.

'I don't want to leave here, Eris, or you,' she said thickly.

Eris set her grinding aside and looked at her. 'You don't want to be with Tierken?'

'I don't want to be in Sarnia. The people stare and there's too much stone.' The complaint sounded childish, even to her own ears.

'You are strong, Kira. You will make a place for yourself there, as you have here.'

'I'll come back and visit you at the end of summer.'

'I ask that you don't,' said Eris.

Kira stared at her in astonishment. 'But—'

'This is my last spring, Kira, and you've seen too much death already. We'll make our farewells now and then you'll remember me as I am this night, our last together.'

Kira sat heavily. 'But how do you know?'

'You're a Healer, Kira, and you ask me how I know?'

'But there are things I can do!' cried Kira, tears starting. 'I can—'

Eris raised her hand. 'We are both of the green and growing. We know of seed fall, understand the uncurling of new leaves, accept the slow creep of decay as death reclaims life. You saw it in the forests and it's here in the allogrenia groves, and in the ice that burns brighter than fire, then slides back to water. It's given to Healers to know when to heal and when to let go.'

Eris cradled Kira's tear-wet face in her hands, as she had on the night Tierken had brought her to Kessom and when she had left. 'I say to you now what I've said before. Give yourself kindness, Kira, and time to heal.' Then she kissed Kira formally on each cheek and hobbled from the room.

The day was more like full summer than spring when Kira and her escort reached Sarnia, and Tierken watched her progress up the path from his vantage point in the lee of the Domain gate. His strategy forbade him greeting her beyond the gate but there were other reasons he waited in the Domain.

The path was already decorated with flowers and black and silver pennants for Laryia's wedding on the morrow. To travel it now with Kira would be to parody the Marriage Walk, and he did not have the stomach for *that*.

Once he had dispatched the Guard to Kessom, word had spread of their mission, as it always did, and crowds had formed, no doubt anticipating seeing the Feailner's *bride-to-be*. Tierken grimaced. Those whose kin she healed might say the gold-eyed Healer had returned or maybe even that the *Tremen Feailner* had but others in Sarnia would grin slyly and say the *Feailner's woman* was back warming the Feailner's bed.

Kira was midway up the path when a cheer began. Tierken had no idea where it had started but he was pleased see that Kira sat straight in the saddle, head held high, and even waved in greeting.

The Domain colors highlighted her fairness and the silver ribbons in the braid around her face glinted like a crown. Her gauntness had been replaced with soft curves too and his blood quickened as she neared.

The party passed through the Domain gate and he watched her slump with relief, and then her face lit up as she saw him, leapt from the mare and bounded to his arms. The sense of her woke a fierce desire and he wondered how in Irid's name he had borne their moons apart *and* how he would bear what was to come.

'I greet you, bondmate,' she said tenderly.

'You look well,' said Tierken. Thank Irid her eyes were gold again. '*Are* you well?'

'How could I not be well, now I'm with my bondmate? And you'll be pleased to know that on the journey here I named the mare Brightwings after the iridescent moths in Allogrenia.'

'A pretty name,' said Tierken, his gaze roving over her. He took her pack from the escort, gripped her elbow, and steered her swiftly across the square.

'Sarnia looks lovely with the flowers and flags,' she said, panting slightly from their pace. 'People seem happy and excited too. It's a wonderful thing to have a wedding so soon after the fighting.'

'Yes it is,' said Tierken, pulling her along the balcony after him, and into her rooms. He slammed the door shut and turned the key, then took her in his arms again. His kisses were so urgent she felt breathless, then he picked her up and carried her to the sleeping-room, where he swiftly removed her jacket and shirt, and loosened the lacings on her trousers. His mouth moved from her neck to her breasts, and she shut her eyes, anticipating his skin next to hers but he did not undress, just clamped her close until his need was satisfied.

Kira's hunger for him remained but he stilled her hands as she unbuttoned his shirt. 'No time for that now,' he said, rising and neatening his clothes. 'I need to outline the wedding schedule so you know what is expected of you tomorrow.' Kira struggled to concentrate, disconcerted by the abruptness of his love-making.

'The celebrations begin with a breakfast banquet I will host with Laryia in the Meeting Hall. All peoples who form the Terak Kirillian or who are allied or treatied to us, are represented. Farid will escort you and Niria will bring you a selection of gowns and help you prepare.

'The marriage ceremony commences at midday at the wall gate. Laryia tells me she's arranged a suitable gown for you. It is customary for the Feailner and his Consort to lead the betrothed couple from the wall gate to the Domain gate with the wedding guests following in order of status. Laryia's partnered me in the past, but obviously that's not possible in this instance, so I'll perform the duty alone. Again, Farid will escort you.

'The Marriage Walk provides an enjoyable spectacle and allows the citizens of Sarnia to offer their best wishes to the couple. The couple pledge before the Marken and then return to the Meeting Hall for the wedding banquet. The celebrations make for a long day and as you've traveled through the night, you should rest now in preparation.'

He nodded to her, in the way she had seen him dismiss servers, and then the door shut behind him, leaving her feeling strangely unsettled. Tierken loved her, had *made love to her*, but she needed time to lie in his arms and speak with him or to simply lie in his arms in silence, knowing he was there.

She dressed again and neatened her hair in the bathing-room. Tierken had responsibility for the wedding preparations and much else to do, apart from being with her, she reminded herself. Once the wedding was over she would have all the time in the world with her bondmate.

142

The realization that she *had* a bondmate washed over her afresh and she laughed with joy.

There was a knock and Laryia appeared with Tresen, and Kira gasped. 'You look so well!' she said, enfolding him in an intense embrace. Tresen was horribly thin and moved with care but apart from that, looked as he always had, and Kira laughed again, in relief this time.

'You look well also, clanmate,' said Tresen, with a broad smile. 'And I congratulate you on your bonding. May your love be as strong and enduring as the alwaysgreen.'

'I wish that your love be as strong and enduring as the alwaysgreen too,' said Laryia, using the Tremen form of congratulations, as she kissed Kira on each cheek. 'Now, I'll leave you two alone, as I know you've had little chance to speak since you came North. And Kira, sometime today Niria will bring the dress you wore to the banquet at Mid-market. I've had it ornamented and a circlet made for your hair.' She smiled warmly. 'You're going to look so beautiful as you lead the Marriage Walk with Tierken.'

'I'm not leading the Marriage Walk with Tierken,' said Kira. 'The Keeper's to partner me.'

Laryia stared at her in astonishment. 'But the Feailner's Consort *always* leads it with him.'

'The morrow belongs to you and Tresen, not to me,' said Kira. 'I'm well content with how Tierken has arranged things.' Laryia nodded but she looked troubled as she left.

'Sit, clanmate, and conserve your strength,' said Kira, as soon as Laryia had gone. 'From what Tierken's told me, the morrow will tax you greatly. And before you get too comfortable, show me that wound.'

'Always the Healer,' grumbled Tresen, as he laboriously pulled off his shirt.

143

'Yes,' said Kira, 'So you know better than to lie to me about your pain. How is your breathing?'

'I won't be sprinting anywhere.'

'No,' she said, probing gently. 'The spear damaged your lungs. Still, you look better than I dared hope.'

'I hadn't realized the healing power of love,' he said soberly, as he struggled his shirt back on. 'Between you and Laryia, I've been extremely fortunate. Your love pulled me back into life and Laryia's love gave me reason to stay.' He paused. 'How is it with you and Tierken?'

'As you see,' said Kira with a smile. 'I love him and we've bonded.'

'But that isn't enough for him, is it?'

Kira faltered. 'What mean you?'

'Tierken's told no one but Laryia you've bonded. The Keeper doesn't even know and he's Tierken's closest friend. And Tierken denies you your rightful place in the Marriage Walk. As his Consort, you should be walking by his side.'

Kira swallowed dryly and Tresen gentled his voice. 'To *fully* accept the kin-link, Tierken must accept *our* customs, Kira. Laryia and I have told him in various ways and at various times that, in Tremen terms, you are as married to him now, as Laryia and I will be to each other by this time on the morrow. But everything he's done so far, or *not* done, tells me he doesn't accept your bonding.'

'Don't say that!'

Tresen's warm hand closed over hers. 'I'm your clanmate, Kira. We grew together and I love you. I have to say it.'

There was a strained silence and it was Kira who broke it. 'You don't understand the enormity of what Tierken did. He demanded that the Terak accept Kasheron's *deserters* back into the city. Sarnia's *full* acceptance of the Tremen and Tierken's *full* acceptance of *me*, will take time. I'm prepared to wait.'

Tresen recalled Caledon saying something similar about his preparedness to wait for Kira, and now Kira said the same thing about Tierken. It seemed the only person not required to be patient was the Northern Feailner.

'Laryia and I won't be leaving for Allogrenia until Terak patrolmen have *secured* it, whatever that means. I'm not sure Kest will be too pleased but I understand Tierken's concerns and obviously I want Laryia safe too. I'm happy to act as Leader on my return, Kira, if that's what the Clancouncil want, but my guess is that no new leader can be appointed until you formally renounced the leadership.'

'I could send a message with you,' suggested Kira.

'I don't think that would be enough.'

'I'll ask Tierken about my visiting Allogrenia then, but I don't think now is a good time,' said Kira. Tresen did not think *any* time would be good for the Northern Feailner, but he held his tongue.

16

Kira did not have much time to speak with Tresen after all because he tired so quickly she helped him back to his rooms. The square was full of richly dressed strangers enjoying the sunshine and she realized Caledon must be somewhere in the Domain too. She longed to see him but people paused in their conversations at her approach and as soon as Tresen was safely in his rooms, she took refuge in hers.

Niria arrived with a platter of food and an armful of gowns. Kira liked a brown one best, not just because its rich color was like terrawood bark, but because it had little metal, but she chose one in the Domain colors of black with silver-metal trim to please Tierken and show her willingness to fit into the Domain as his bondmate.

She looked forward to his pleasure at her choice when he came later and to telling him about the dwinhir hatchlings above Kessom. She perched on her bed to watch the Silvercades pass through their glorious hues of pink and orange, then cool blue as the sun slipped below the horizon, but Tierken did not appear.

He would be busy with the wedding preparations, she told herself, or the guests in the square, but disappointment sat like a stone in her stomach and Tresen's words haunted her. Tresen disliked Tierken but Kira did not believe it colored his judgements but rather, like most of the Protectors, Tresen did not understand the complexities of being the Northern Feailner. Tierken must deal with the Marken and traders; the disparate habits of the Terak, Kirs,

Illians, Kessomis and now the Tremen; and the alliances and treaties with the Tain and Ashmiri.

Nor did Tresen understand the *depth* of animosity for Kasheron in the North. It alone was reason enough to keep their bonding secret, although it made her uneasy Tierken had failed to tell Farid.

Unease may have caused her to sleep poorly or the change from the crisp herb-scented air of Eris's house, but she was dressed and waiting when the Keeper arrived to collect her at dawn. It was easier to dismiss her fears in the clear light of day and the Keeper seemed genuinely pleased to see her.

'It gladdens me to have you safely back,' he said warmly, as he gripped her hands. Kira had barely seen him during the fighting, but his skill had kept the Haelen supplied with herbs and helpers, and she was glad he was to guide her through this important day. 'I beg your pardon I didn't have a chance to greet you yesterday,' he said, as they made their way along the balcony. 'Between Laryia's wedding, opening up *Kasheron's Quarter*, and rebuilding the southern Rehan, it's been a busy time.'

'By contrast, I've been very lazy in Kessom,' said Kira lightly.

'I'm sure that's not the case. I've heard reports you gathered and shared your healing in your usual generous manner.'

Kira flushed at the compliment and glanced sideways at him as she debated whether to tell him of the bonding. The Owl Fountain gleamed, the sky was clear, and a happy day stretched ahead filled with celebrations for Tresen and Laryia, people Kira loved.

The Keeper smiled. 'What is it?' he asked.

Groups of ornately garbed men and women moved towards the Meeting Hall too and Kira lowered her voice. 'Tierken and I have bonded.'

The Keeper jerked to a stop. 'Bonded?'

Kira laughed, unable to contain her excitement. 'It's the Tremen equivalent of Terak marriage.'

Others edged past them and they went on. 'But when?' whispered Farid.

'When he came to Kessom after the fighting. Aren't you going to congratulate me?'

'May you have a long life with clear skies,' said the Keeper, still looking stunned. 'I would have thought—'

'I think Tierken's only told Laryia and Tresen. Few in Kessom know either or the Tremen. He wants to give Sarnia time to get used to their kin coming North again, without the added complication of describing bonding, but I wanted you to know.'

There was no time for further speech as servers appeared to escort them to their seats. Kira eagerly scanned the room for Caledon until the Keeper reminded her that Talliel was neither part of the Terak Kirillian nor joined by treaty or alliance. Tresen was not at the banquet either, which was not surprising given his fragile health.

Guests streamed in, the darker Kirs; the tall, muscular Illians and Teraks; and the slightly built Kessomis. King Adris was seated close to Tierken and even Ashmiri were there, though not Uthlin. Kira took her seat and the Tremen Protector Leaders came straight to her table to greet her formally, and Kira had to blink hard to clear her vision.

Tierken did not rise to speak until well into the meal, and then he spoke only briefly. He welcomed the Terak peoples in turn, listing the Tremen after the Kirs and Illians, but before the Kessomis, then those allied with or treatied to the Terak, and finished with a toast to Laryia and congratulations on her imminent marriage. Then he sat down.

Kira tried to catch his eye, but he did not look in her direction and once the guests had finished their meal they began to drift back out into the sunny square and the Keeper escorted Kira out too. She yearned to speak to Tierken but knew the Keeper had many matters to attend to more important than keeping her company, and she thanked him and returned to her rooms.

Niria appeared soon afterwards to help her into the new gown and dress her hair. 'The Domain path is already crowded,' she said excitedly, as she tweaked the green gown into place. 'You look like Queen Kiraon herself, come back to life,' she added with a smile. 'It's said she was slight built with fair hair and gold eyes and favored green and gold too.'

Kira felt more treacherous than queenly as Niria replaced the silver and black ribbons in her braid with green ribbons and positioned the gold, gem-set circlet on her head. Kira just hoped the Tremen who witnessed Laryia and Tresen's wedding understood the reason she wore metal.

The Keeper's eyes widened when he saw her, and he continued to glance sideways at her as they made their way out the Domain gate and turned along a side street. 'It is considered ill fortune to use the Domain path to descend on the day of a wedding,' he said as they walked.

The narrow street they used was crowded but the Guard who preceded and followed them, meant that others gave way. Black and silver ribbons and banners hung from windows in honor of the Feailner's sister, and Kira smiled at the children who peered through open shutters. 'The beautiful Tremen Feailner,' said Adris as he fell into step beside her. 'You look very well indeed.'

Kira flushed as his black eyes roved over her. 'King Adris, it's good to see you once more. I am very relieved you escaped the fighting unscathed.'

'You doubt my sword skill?'

The heat in Kira's face increased. 'By no means. You've been formally introduced to the Domain Keeper?' she asked, gesturing to Farid.

'Of course,' said Adris, his gaze on her.

'I've yet to see the Lord Caledon,' said Kira. 'Is he in front or behind us?'

'It's hard to tell in this crowd. You'll see him at the banquet though. I know he's keen to speak with you.'

'And I with him,' said Kira. 'Do you know when he intends to return home?'

'I think that depends on you.'

Kira was aware of the Keeper's tension and forced a smile. 'I have bonded with the Terak Feailner so the Domain is now my home. Bonding is the Tremen form of marriage,' she added.

'Not quite, from what Lord Caledon tells me,' said Adris pleasantly. 'But I will pass on your happy news. I'm sure he will wish to congratulate you in person.' Then, with a nod, he lengthened his stride and drew ahead.

They reached the wall and made their way along in its cool shadow to the gate. A long line of dignitaries had already assembled but the Keeper escorted Kira past them and their conversations faltered. 'They admire your gown,' he murmured.

'But not my bloodline, Keeper.'

'Call me Farid,' he said with a smile. 'You look exquisite. It's just that Sarnia's not used to gold that lives.'

150

'What about the Feailner's eyes?'

He cocked an eyebrow. 'Now which Feailner would that be?'

'Which would you prefer?' asked Kira, her tension lessening.

'It's hard to choose. They're both my favorites.'

Kira laughed at ease again. 'Are Tierken, Laryia and Tresen late, or are they hiding in the crowd?' she asked, peering about.

'They wait in the Marriage House behind the stables. It was built for the happy couple to rest in while the Sarnia Guard persuade their guests to line up in order of importance. This usually takes some time. Guests are perplexed to discover they're the twelfth most important person in Sarnia, not the sixth. No one likes moving back.'

'Does that mean *we're* the most important people in Sarnia?' asked Kira lightly, as she and Farid took up their positions at the top of the line.

'Indeed, it does, after the Feailner, who leads, and the pledged couple, of course. I come next, as Keeper of the Domain, then the highly placed members of the Kir, Illian and Kessomi communities follow. But because this is the marriage of the Feailner's *sister*, those we're allied to must be slotted in too. King Adris is placed highly because of the renewed friendship between the Tain and the Terak. The only marriage more important than this will be the marriage of the Feailner himself.' Farid faltered. 'I beg your pardon, Kira. I didn't mean—'

'I know you didn't,' Kira reassured him.

The people behind fell silent as they craned their necks to the left, and Kira and Farid followed suit. Then a cheer went up as Tierken walked slowly forward, clad in the

151

Domain black and silver, a circlet of silver bright against his dark hair.

Laryia and Tresen followed, and the cheering increased as they took up their places behind Tierken. Laryia sparkled in blue, her beauty heightened by her radiant smile, and Tresen wore the Domain black and silver, but he was pale, and Kira watched him anxiously. There was a brief hiatus as black-clad music-makers took up position, then with a clash of thumb cymbals, the Marriage Walk began.

Bells joined the cymbals, then pipes, soft drums and thumbelins, the tinkling music rippling in a joyous wave that carried them up the path. Flowers rained down, thrown by the crowd, and Kira laughed in delight. Those gathered along the way cried *long life*, *clear skies*, and *burn bright*, wishes for happiness and prosperity that Farid said came from their herding past.

Once the procession had passed, the bystanders fell in behind, following the wedding guests up to the Domain gates. Here the Marken stood to either side of Rosham, with the city's trader leaders gathered behind them. With a final clash of cymbals, the music stilled and the crowd hushed as Tierken went forward and took his place in the midst of the Marken, turning to face the crowd and forcing Rosham to move sideways or stare at his back.

Then Marken Milsin stepped forward and in a sonorous voice, outlined the gravity of the step the couple were to take. Milsin fell silent and then Tresen and Laryia turned to face each other. Tresen's pallor had increased but he spoke steadily, completing his pledge and as Laryia began hers, Kira glanced beyond them to Tierken and smiled. He looked directly at her and their eyes met but he did not smile back.

152

Laryia finished her pledge to love and live together until death, then Tresen took the pledge bracelet from Laryia's right wrist and slipped it onto her left one. The crowd erupted with cheers but Kira barely heard them. Despite the warm day, she shivered. Tresen might be right about Tierken after all.

17

The servers had been busy since the breakfast banquet and the Meeting Hall was now festooned with flowers, silver chimes, and black ribbons. The tables were set in crisp white; metal platters and goblets gleamed in the light of lattice-worked lanterns; and perfumed candles lent the air a sweet scent. The seating order was much as it had been at the Mid-market banquet, with the addition of Laryia and Tresen to the top table, and Kira and Farid again at the closest lower table, along with Adris, Caledon, and the more important of the lesser traders.

Conversations hummed amidst the clang of metal, but Kira's attention was on Tierken. Just one tender glance from him would reassure her all was well, but he conversed with two, silver-haired trader leaders. Tierken wanted to marry in the Terak way and having to watch Laryia do so must have been hard, but the more she considered his coldness, the more frightened she grew.

'Could you grant me a favor, Farid?' she said eventually.

'Of course.'

'Could you change places with the Lord Caledon for a moment? I need to speak with him.'

'By all means.'

He rose and whispered to Caledon, and Caledon came and settled beside her. 'You look very well, Kira,' he said. 'Your time in Kessom seems to have agreed with you.' He paused. 'Adris tells me congratulations are in order.'

'Yes. Tierken and I have bonded,' she said and managed to smile. Telling Farid just a short time ago had brought her joy but now doubt gnawed.

Caledon inclined his head. 'Then I wish you both long life and happiness.' Kira said nothing and Caledon considered her calmly. 'Given you are now Tierken's Consort, I'm puzzled you're not sitting with your bondmate at the top table.'

'I think the Terak have enough to deal with, without adding a bondmate,' said Kira lightly.

'*You* think? Or *he* thinks?'

Kira had trouble meeting Caledon's eyes. 'We both think.'

'When exactly is he planning to acknowledge you then?'

Kira smiled but her face felt wooden. 'I don't know. We haven't discussed it.'

Caledon smiled too and sipped his drink. 'I admit I was surprised when Adris told me your news. I'd heard nothing of it from the Marken, or the trader leaders, or even the Tremen Protectors. If I had bonded with you, Kira, the whole world would have known by now.'

Kira flushed. 'Tierken still has difficulties in Sarnia,' she said, but the excuse sounded unconvincing even in her own ears.

'That might be true, but I don't think it's the reason he denies you your rightful place at his side. I think it is as we've discussed: that he doesn't accept who or what you are.'

'We've bonded,' repeated Kira stubbornly.

'I've no doubt *you* have bonded with him, Kira, but I see no evidence *he* has bonded with you.' He glanced beyond her to the top table. 'Perhaps it is best I return to my seat.'

Kira caught Caledon's hand, despite knowing Tierken watched them. 'Pledge me you won't leave Sarnia without saying goodbye. I couldn't bear it if you suddenly disappeared.'

'As you've chosen the Terak Feailner over the Tallien Placidien, I can't see it would make any difference.'

It was the first time Caledon had alluded to the interruption of their burgeoning love. His clear grey eyes held none of Tierken's hardness but Kira suddenly understood how much she had hurt him. She dropped her head, but his fingers gently raised it. 'I pledge not to leave without proper farewell on condition that you pledge not to stay with a man who brings you no happiness.'

'I've bonded with him!'

'And Miken's explained *exactly* what that means.'

Kira's eyes flashed. 'I'm not faithless!'

Caledon's voice dropped to a harsh whisper. 'It's not *your* commitment that concerns me. The test of love is trust, Kira. Where there's no trust, love fails. If all Tierken needs is more time to return your trust, then I will leave you gladly, knowing you've found happiness, for if anyone deserves happiness, Kira, it's you. But I don't believe it will be so and I don't want you to stay here in *misery* under the misapprehension you've failed or that it's your fault.'

Tierken's gaze on them was now so intense it drew the attention of others. 'People are staring,' she muttered.

'I'm waiting for your answer.'

'I pledge,' said Kira, desperate to end the interest they generated.

Caledon rose and, with a small bow, made his way back to his seat, then Farid returned and launched into an animated description of how the rest of the night would proceed. Kira kept her gaze on his face as if fascinated by his words but she struggled not to panic. Caledon had not

156

minced his words and what he had said fed the black hole of her doubts.

She wanted Tierken close, the reassurance of his touch and of the smile that was just for her, but she did not trust herself to look at him, fearing his expression would confirm Tresen and Caledon's warnings.

The music-makers began, and conversations hushed as Laryia and Tresen made their way onto the dance floor, then applause broke out as they started to dance, but Tresen was so uncertain in his movements Kira feared he would collapse.

The dance steps were slow and intricate, and the applause fell into the same rhythm, then Tierken made his way down. Kira's heart pounded but he walked past her without a glance and, with a bow to Tresen, took Laryia's hand. It was Tresen who turned towards Kira, so pale that Kira hurriedly met him halfway across the floor. Her lack of familiarity with the steps did not matter because Tresen barely had the strength to move and as the Marken and the trader leaders led their wives onto the dance floor, Kira eased Tresen out the door into the cooler evening air.

'Are you in pain from the wound or are your lungs troubling you?' she asked, as he sagged against the wall.

'Pain,' gasped Tresen. 'It's been . . . a long day.'

'I can solve that,' said Kira, busy with his jacket buttons.

Tresen's hand closed over hers. 'No. I feel . . . a little better now.'

'I know how you feel, Tresen, my hand's burning through your shirt. And I don't intend your special night to be ruined.'

Kira slid her hand through the openings in his jacket and shirt and was immediately engulfed in fire, and then she was back in the evening air and Tresen supported *her*. He gently brought his forehead to hers. 'I've never decided whether you bear the most wonderful gift, Tremen Leader Feailner Kiraon of Kashclan, or the most terrible curse,' he said softly.

'Definitely the first, clanmate,' she said, still dizzy.

The door opened and Tierken appeared. 'Your wife wonders where you are, Tremen Healer Tresen.'

'I thank you, Feailner,' said Tresen, but did not release Kira. 'All right now?'

'Yes,' said Kira. 'Enjoy the rest of your wedding day.' Tresen bowed to Tierken and disappeared back inside but Tierken remained where he was, his expression cold. 'Tresen wasn't feeling well,' said Kira. 'I was—'

'I saw what you were doing.'

Tierken's inference was plain. 'Tresen's my clanmate. He's—'

'Married to my sister, a pledge which is binding, unlike the arrangements the Tremen make. I know you're ignorant of the difference, Kira, but I didn't realize Tresen was too.'

Kira's anger woke. 'Are you suggesting—'

'You disrupted the last celebration I hosted here but I'd hoped you'd matured since then or at least learned some manners, but it seems I'm to be disappointed on both counts.'

He turned on his heel and the door slammed behind him but Kira wrenched it open again and stormed back into the hall. The dance floor was crowded, with Laryia and Tresen now leading thread-the-leaves. Tierken had paused to speak to a beautiful, black-haired woman on the edge of the dance floor, but Farid, Caledon and Adris were all unpartnered and she strode over.

'Lord Caledon,' she said. 'I've shared rain, wind, and thunder with you, but never a dance. Would you do me the honor?'

'The honor and pleasure are mine,' said Caledon rising.

But Kira had only been dancing with Caledon a short while before she realized she had made a mistake. His sweet spice scent woke memories of their time together and made the temptation to stay in the Shelter of his arms overwhelming. *If I had bonded with you, Kira, the whole world would have known by now.*

Kira had intended to ask Adris to dance next, then Farid, determined not to repeat the humiliation of the Mid-market banquet, but she was so unnerved by the feelings Caledon roused that she excused herself as soon as the dance ended and hastened back to her rooms.

She locked the door and sagged against it, eyes closed, then settled at the table and forced herself to consider every unpalatable thing that had happened since her return to Sarnia. And what was horribly clear was that, apart from the day of her arrival, Tierken had shunned her. Even worse, tonight he had made his contempt for bonding abundantly clear. But why ask her to bond if he despised it?

She thought back to that special moment. They had been in the shelter-hut in the Silvercades when the nightmare had woken her. Tierken had wanted to know about the dream, but she had been too angry to tell him, and then they argued over Caledon. Her breath caught. Surely Tierken had not bonded to keep her from Caledon?

The idea was so shocking she struggled even to consider it. But even if it *had* been Tierken's motivation, it did not mean he did not love her, it meant he did not *trust* her, and she already knew that. And yet . . . Kira brought a shaking hand to her mouth. *Shunning* her was not about a lack of trust, it was about a lack of *love*.

She recalled how the patrolmen had bragged of having deceived their wives. The patrols were long too, and the maps showed small settlements scattered north of the Sarsalin. If the patrolmen had lovers there then Tierken probably did too. She considered the beautiful woman Tierken had been speaking with earlier. He likely had lovers in Sarnia as well. He was handsome and his status as Feailner made him desirable.

Kira's stomach churned as she considered her options. She must either wait for his trust to grow and with it, his need for other lovers to diminish, or break the bond. She rose and went to the window. Kashclan did not break their bondings. There were many in the Kashclan longhouse who had never bonded, and none who had bonded twice. Bonding was not entered into lightly and *never* without love and she *did* love Tierken even if he no longer loved her.

The Silvercades were bright in the moonlight. A full moon, she realized dully, the first of summer and then she faltered. It was Turning in Allogrenia! Was that why Tresen and Laryia had chosen to marry now? Turning meant she was eighteen and Kandor would have been fourteen. Tears slid down her cheeks. His loss was akin to physical pain and she thought of the others who lay beneath the alwaysgreens, robbed of their chance to live and love.

Her father had accused her of being untrustworthy, of not completing her undertakings, of failing her duties, and she had failed in many duties since: protecting Kandor, sharing her knowing with Kest, seeking the Clancouncil's permission to leave Allogrenia, keeping trust with Caledon.

Was she to fail in the bonding too, the most important pledge of her life?

18

It was dawn before Tierken farewelled the last of his guests. Laryia and Tresen had been sent off to their rooms much earlier with the traditional storm of clapping and throws of white and red petals, and some of the older guests had gone to their beds soon after, leaving the dance floor to those of fewer seasons.

Tierken had overheard comments about Kira's beauty all day. It had been Laryia's special day and his sister had looked exquisite, but Kira's eyes, fairness, and the gold in her hair and gown had set her apart. If she were his wife he could have proudly shown her off, but he could hardly flaunt his *woman* in such a way. Instead, he'd had to watch her on Farid's arm and then endure her dancing with the Tallien. He would be glad when the man was back in Talliel, despite his aid.

Tierken paused outside his rooms and rolled his shoulders. His nerves were as taut as during the fighting, when attack could come from anywhere at any time and often did. Laryia's rooms were quiet and Tierken doubted Tresen had the strength to bring his sister joy this night. It was ironic that Laryia had married a man too injured to take her in love, and he had taken a woman in love who refused to marry him. Irid must have muddled up his and his sister's fates, he concluded sourly.

As soon as the wedding guests departed Sarnia, he would send men south to secure the route to Allogrenia. Laryia and her husband would journey around Watchan Spur, for it was dangerous for horses to cross the Azurcades, and he would need to consider how Terak patrols were to be accommodated in the Tremen lands. He certainly was not leaving Laryia's safety in the hands of Protectors.

Kira's door suddenly opened and he spun and dropped into a crouch, his hand flashing to the empty place at his belt. She was dressed for riding, he saw as he rose, the close-fitting dark green shirt and trousers reminding him exactly where her curves were. The ornate crown-like braid had been replaced with a simpler one that kept the hair from her eyes and highlighted the fine planes of her face.

'I bid you a good morning, bondmate,' she said evenly, and Tierken grimaced.

'I'd rather you didn't call me that.'

'Then I bid you a good morning, *Feailner*.'

'Call me Tierken, as you usually do.'

'Then I bid you a good morning, *Tierken*. Will you join me for a ride?'

'I thought you would be too tired to ride. I presumed it was why you breached custom by leaving the celebrations before the married couple.'

Her eyes darkened but her tone remained the same. 'I beg *their* pardon and *yours* for failing to follow Terak customs.' She nodded briefly and strode off.

'I will ride,' Tierken called after her.

Kira made no reply. She almost regretted the invitation as she made her way swiftly across the square to the stables and she had saddled Brightwings *and* Kalos before Tierken appeared. He had changed into the browns and greens of a patrolman and donned his weapons.

They rode the Rehan, heading east until they reached the Steelwater, then turning south along its banks. Tierken rode by her side, but said little, even when she asked him direct questions and Kira soon wished she had ridden alone.

At least Brightwings seemed to enjoy the excursion and as she chaffed at the bit, Kira let the mare have her head. She sprang away, and Kira crouched low in the saddle, urging her to greater and greater speed. Tierken shouted something but she ignored him, the world an exhilarating blur of river water and emerald grass that scoured away her frustrated longing and then Kalos pounded alongside and Tierken leaned over and grabbed her rein.

He brought the mare to a violent stop, jumped down and wrenched Kira from the saddle. 'Don't—ever—do—that—again!' he shouted.

Tierken panted with fury and Kira with shock at being so abruptly unhorsed. 'Why not?' she shouted back, refusing to step back as he confronted her.

'If she went down, she'd be killed and so would you!'

'Ryn says she's sure-footed!'

'Nothing's sure-footed at that speed! I thought you'd outgrown your recklessness!'

'I've *never* been reckless!'

'Jumping from trees, jumping from windows, going to Kessom in snow-melt, taking pain. The list goes on. Shall I continue?'

'Don't bother.' She snatched the reins back but Tierken's hand fastened on her arm. She knew some of his anger stemmed from the wedding, but her blood was up too, and she wrenched herself free. 'I'm *bonded* to you, Tierken, not married! You don't *own* me!'

'That's not what marriage is!'

'It's not what bonding is either!'

'I want you to pledge you won't risk yourself like that again!'

164

'Pledge? You're keen on pledges, aren't you, except your own.'

'My own?'

'Our bonding!'

His expression of contempt was fleeting but unmistakable and she drew a steadying breath. 'I know you don't understand Tremen customs, Tierken. I know you think because a bond can be broken, it *will* be broken. But it's no more likely to be broken than a marriage. I've listened to your men boast of the women they've taken to their beds while they're away from their wives, but when I bonded to you, I undertook to take no other lover and to spend the rest of my days with you, and I meant it.'

'I suppose that's why, on the night of my sister's wedding, I find her husband in your arms,' he sneered.

'Tresen was in so much pain I feared he would collapse,' she said furiously. 'I took his pain so he could enjoy the rest of his wedding day. And as you know, *Feailner*, taking pain leaves a residue of illness that needs time to pass.' She swung herself back onto Brightwings. 'Tresen's all I've got left, *Feailner,* and I love him. And I *won't* beg your pardon for that!'

Kira resisted the urge to spite Tierken by galloping Brightwings at high speed all the way back to Sarnia and while she was too angry to care whether she was flung to her death, she did care whether Brightwings was injured or killed. If Tierken really believed she would take her *clanmate* as a lover, *on his wedding day*, then spending even another day in the Domain was pointless.

She stopped at the Haelen, relieved to see it was quiet and the pallets empty, and felt a rare sense of satisfaction.

Sarnia had healing again! Arlen was busy extracting a large splinter from a woodcutter's hand, and she waited while he salved the wound and sent the man on his way.

'It's good to see you, Tremen Leader,' said Arlen with a bow.

'It's good to see you too,' said Kira with feeling. Arlen reminded her of the simple days in Allogrenia before everything had changed. 'Can you tell me where the Tremen are billeted?' she asked. The Proctector leaders at the breakfast banquet had reminded her of how remiss she had been as Tremen Leader. She did not even know how many Protectors were in Sarnia.

'I know where Protector Leader Dendrin is,' said Arlen, 'but the others might be beyond the gates. The Terak Feailner assigned us on leave until the next full moon, but now you're back, surely it's your commands we'll follow?'

'I'm in agreement with the Northern Feailner's orders *for the present*. The Protectors need time to rest and recover before they return to Allogrenia.'

'There might not be many to return,' said Arlen slowly.

Kira faltered, dismayed she had failed to ask about the Tremen dead. 'How many Protectors were killed, Arlen?'

'I don't know exactly, Tremen Leader. I wasn't thinking of those who can't return but of those who might not want to.'

Kira eyed him and then smiled as he reddened. 'What's her name, Arlen?'

'Resa. She's the sister of Patrolman Rein, whose family I'm billeted with. I thought I could work here in the Haelen and make my trade that way, *if* you think there's sufficient need of healing in Sarnia.'

'There's sufficient need for many Healers,' said Kira with feeling. She still found the notion of accepting trade repellent, but given how the city functioned, probably inevitable.

'Protector Leader Dendrin says Terak will go to Allogrenia too,' said Arlen. 'Will they accompany you on your return, Tremen Leader, or go later?'

'I am bonded to the Terak Feailner and will remain here.'

Arlen gasped. 'But you're the Tremen Leader!'

'Healer Tresen will likely replace me *if* the Clancouncil judges him the best Healer.'

'*You* are our *best* Healer,' insisted Arlen.

Kira moved towards the door. 'When you see Protector Leader Dendrin, please send him to me at the Domain. I need to speak with him.'

'Yes, of course, Tremen Leader.'

Kira had not been back in her rooms long when there was a knock at the door. She expected it to be Dendrin but it was Tierken. He was still in high temper but Kira was determined not to continue the quarrel. She wanted to know about the Tremen dead, but before she could ask, she realized that no one in Allogrenia even knew the fighting had ended.

'They won't know for at least two more moons,' confirmed Tierken.

'But they will fear they must deal with a victorious Shargh with too few Protectors to defend them,' cried Kira, pacing up and down.

'Blame Kasheron for taking his followers so far south,' said Tierken with a shrug. 'It's a long journey from here.

But I didn't come—'

Kira swung back to him. 'How many Protectors were killed in the fighting?'

'I can't tell you.'

'But you know how many Terak were killed?'

'Of course,' said Tierken impatiently.

'And Adris knows how many Tain died?'

'I don't know the Protectors like I know my own men,' he said tersely. 'After Pekrash died, we combined forces, and when the fighting came North, Lord Caledon led the Tremen.'

'So Caledon knows who was killed and where they're buried?'

'He would know who was killed but we followed Terak funeral practices.'

Kira's mouth dried. 'Which are?' she asked hoarsely.

'Burning.'

Kira had to grip the chair. 'But that means their voices have been silenced forever,' she whispered.

'The flames loose the spirit to the sky and so the spirits of the dead are all around us. We couldn't risk more lives by seeking groves and digging graves.'

Kira was so distressed Tierken gave in to the urge to take her in his arms. The feel of her flooded his senses and he closed his eyes. He carried a residual weariness from the long days and nights of fighting, of not knowing which of his men would die next, of not knowing whether *he* would live to see another dawn, and he was tired of fighting *her*.

He wanted her safe in Sarnia, her status assured, and a return to the predictable routine of patrolling and administering the city. But to have these things, he must continue his stinking strategy. He released her and stepped back.

'Stay with me, Tierken. We've only come together once since we bonded.'

'That's your choice. If I had brought you back from Kessom as my wife, we would be sharing rooms like Laryia and Tresen. As it is . . .' He managed to shrug. 'I've explained that Sarnia doesn't understand or accept bonding.'

'That didn't stop us being together before.'

He shrugged again. 'It was ill considered. Since I've worked more closely with the trader leaders, I've come to understand more of the . . . subtleties of the city.'

Kira's chin came up. 'I don't think Sarnia's *subtleties* are the reason,' she said. 'I think it's you.'

It sounded like the Tallien's words again. '*You* think or the *Lord Caledon* thinks?' he demanded. 'He's expressed such sentiments about me before and for obvious reasons. We both know he desires you, but what really intrigues me is whether *you* desire him.'

'I'm bonded to *you*!'

'A temporary arrangement you can break when you feel like it.'

The gold drained from her eyes to leave them a moss green. 'You can break the bonding too, Tierken,' she said thickly. 'If you can't tolerate the embarrassment of a Tremen bondmate, if you don't want the seed of the contemptible Kasheron, if my gold eyes and Healer habits create too many difficulties for you as Feailner, if you want other lovers, if you no longer love me—'

Tierken turned back to the door, unable to bear the look on her face. 'Lord Caledon will be able to supply a list of the Tremen dead,' he said curtly. 'I'll ensure he prepares one before he departs. He rides out on the morrow with King Adris. If you wish to farewell either of them, be at the stables at dawn.'

19

When Kira arrived at the stables the next morning, she was surprised to see two Terak patrols mounted and waiting, as well as the King's Guard. The horses tossed their heads and stomped as Tierken conversed with Adris, and Kira stared at the patrols worriedly. They suggested the Sarsalin was still under Shargh threat and if it were, the danger might extend to Allogrenia.

Caledon stood a little apart, busy with his mount's harness but Kira went to Adris first and bowed. 'I wish you a safe journey to Maraschin, King Adris.'

Adris's black eyes held hers as he returned her bow. 'And I wish the new Lady of the Domain a long and happy reign.'

Kira nodded, avoiding Tierken's gaze, but as she went to turn away he handed her a scroll. 'The lists you requested from the Lord Caledon.'

Kira managed to thank him and went to Caledon. 'You have the lists, I see,' he said, as he clipped on his bow and quiver.

'How many, Caledon?'

'Forty-eight.'

She briefly closed her eyes as she thought of the empty chairs in the longhouses and of the never ending grief that would follow, and now Caledon rode away from Sarnia's safety. 'Do you go to Talliel now or Maraschin?' she asked hoarsely.

'To Maraschin first where we'll leave the horses. Then I'll continue on foot with the patrols over the Azurcades to the Southern Forests.'

Kira blinked. 'Tierken's sending patrols to Allogrenia?'

'Yes. He prepares the forest for his sister's arrival and given I'm acquainted with Protector Commander Kest and the Clanleaders, he accepted my offer to ease what could be a difficult meeting.' Caledon swung himself into the saddle. 'I assumed he'd discussed these matters with you, given you're the Tremen Feailner and his bondmate.'

Kira said nothing and he gentled his voice. 'Is there a message you would have me pass on to your kin?'

'Only that I'm safe and happy.'

He glanced in Tierken's direction and leaned over his horse's shoulder. 'I will tell them that if you wish. Remember your pledge to me,' he added softly.

Kira nodded. 'You'll come back to Sarnia one day, won't you, Caledon?'

'If the stars will it.' His grey eyes held hers. 'May the grace of Aeris keep you safe, Kira.'

She nodded and saw Caledon straighten in the saddle as Tierken approached, stopped behind her, and rested his hand on her shoulder. 'A safe journey, Lord Caledon.'

'I thank you, Feailner,' he said, and inclined his head. Kira watched the party move off, wishing with all her heart she was going with them but the Domain gate clanged shut and Tierken's hand steered her back across the square.

'You should have told me you were sending men to Allogrenia,' she said.

'You knew I had to ensure Laryia's safety and it made sense to accept Lord Caledon's offer to act as an intermediary. According to him, he's trusted by your people. Is that not the case?'

'As the Tremen Leader, I should have been told,' she said stubbornly.

172

'Tremen Healer Tresen or whoever your people choose, will shortly take on the role, and then—' He stopped as Tharin approached. 'Yes, Guard Leader?'

'Tremen Protector Dendrin is at the gate. He requests speech with the Tremen Leader.'

'Show him to the Meeting Hall,' said Tierken, before Kira could speak. 'Why would Dendrin seek you?' he asked her.

'I requested him to come. I want to know where my people are billeted in the city, how many intend to stay, and how they envisage making trade to live. And I've never thanked them for the sacrifices they made in volunteering.'

'I have a full list of where the Tremen are billeted and at last count forty-one were definite in their plans to stay, at least for another season. They will be accommodated in the houses in Kasheron's Quarter as soon as they are complete.

'Some have expressed interest in becoming patrolmen and others already put their woodworking skills to use with the woodwrights in the Rehan where many houses were lost. As their Commander, I thanked them for their service.'

'I still need to speak with him,' persisted Kira.

'If you wish,' said Tierken. 'I must meet with Marin now to plan the next patrol.'

Kira looked at him in dismay. 'You're not going before Tresen and Laryia leave, are you?'

'I must ensure the eastern route over the Sarsalin is clear, but I'll return before the full moon to properly farewell them,' he said, and strode away.

Dendrin simply reiterated what Tierken had said and, feeling superfluous, Kira went down to the Haelen, but for once, no one had scalded or cut themselves, woken inexplicably wracked with pain, or eaten something Meros had cursed. Arlen was in the Herbery grinding sorren with a pretty brown-eyed woman, and it was clear neither of them welcomed her company. Scowling, she decided she might as well continue her interrupted exploration of the Rehan Valley.

Guard Farsrin and Storsil's mounts cantered at Brightwings' heels but the Steelwater's gleam and the flash of water birds that broke from its reeds soothed her frustrations. The people she passed ceased their work to bow and Kira waved back. She did not want bows, but it was better than being spat at, she conceded. She enjoyed Brightwings' warm horse smell, and while the Rehan was not heavily treed like Allogrenia, the air was full of birdsong. The day was sunny, the fighting finished, and she was with the man she loved. She refused to think any further.

They came to the first of the burned houses as shadows striped the valley. The smell of charred timber took her back to the Bough, to the horror of the inferno, and to all that had followed, and she brought Brightwings to a halt. They were not far from the valley's mouth and her thoughts went to Allogrenia and her long-neglected duties there.

Brightwings moved restlessly but Kira held her steady. Half of her yearned to gallop south, the other half for the Shelter of Tierken's arms.

'It will be full dark before we reach the city if we don't return now, Lady,' said Farsrin eventually. Kira turned Brightwings north, but it took her almost to the wall gate to shake off the feelings of bleakness.

She was surprised to find Tierken lounging at the table in her rooms, and for the first time since her return to Sarnia, he seemed relaxed. No doubt Caledon's departure had restored his good humor, she thought cynically, as she swung off her pack.

'How far did you ride?' he asked.

'To the burned houses.'

'We're in the process of rebuilding what was destroyed, as are the Tain. No doubt your people are too.'

'If they are, I won't have the chance to find out.'

'Not for a little while,' he agreed, taking a handful of nuts from the dish on the table. 'But Terak and Tremen patrols will journey back and forth and, in time, the route will be safer. Then you can visit.'

'I thought you had defeated the Shargh,' said Kira, irritated by Tierken's smooth assumption of control over her.

'Most of the Cashgar and Weshargh warriors were killed, but the Soushargh took little part in the fighting, and even a defeated people will attack if they deem themselves stronger than their quarry,' he said, starting on the nuts.

'If the Cashgar and Weshargh men are dead, what happens to their families?'

'I have no idea and nor do I care. The Shargh chose their murderous path and slaughtered our women, children and the old, not to mention our men. If their folk now die too then maybe Irid has a sense of justice.'

Kira thought of Jesa and Jesin but she also thought of the Shargh children. 'Are your gods so cruel that they punish the innocent?'

'I didn't come here to discuss the Shargh or our gods,' he said, rubbing the nut crumbs from his hands.

'What did you come here for?'

175

'To see you,' he said softly, coming to her. 'To have time together before I go south.'

Kira bit back a sarcastic remark about him being *ill considered*. His nearness woke her need of him but she eyed him warily. He seemed to move easily between argument and love-making, while every quarrel added to her doubts. His arms came around her, making her feel safe as they always did, and she closed her eyes, shutting out her fears as he dusted her face with kisses.

His love-making was as gentle as in their early days, healing the anger and uncertainty of the past moon but as she lay in his arms afterwards, listening to the strong beat of his heart, her uneasiness crept back.

How long before her refusal to bend to his will ignited his anger again? Until he remembered she was Kasheron's cursed seed? Until he tired of her for ever?

Tierken was gone when Kira woke and she rolled over and inhaled his scent from the cover. She should be used to the briefness of their times together but she found it increasingly difficult. To make matters worse, even when Tierken *was* in the Domain, his disdain for the bond meant she mostly slept alone. She envied Tresen and Laryia in the rooms next door. They seemed in perfect accord but maybe Laryia's love for Tresen would fail in time too.

She breakfasted quickly and made her way to the Wastes. At least Tierken's absence gave her time to weed Queen Kiraon's garden. The day was sunny and despite the dumps of refuse, Kira delighted in her time there. It was the only place in Sarnia where the lush greenness allowed her to pretend she was Allogrenia. She could even ignore the Guards' bored shufflings *most of the time*. Stone and woodwrights passed by, carting tools and building supplies, and the sound of hammers and saws reminded Kira that one day the Wastes would truly be Kasheron's Quarter.

The weather remained fine and she worked until dusk each day, her back aching and her hands blistered, but her mind blessedly empty and slowly, Queen Kiraon's garden re-emerged from the tangle. Sometimes when she worked, she paused to imagine a young and healthy alwaysgreen in place of the stump, encircled by a beautifully carved stone seat like those in the Domain, and the surrounding terraces alive with brightly flowering herbs.

There was no reason why the streets in Kasheron's Quarter could not be clothed in greenery too, and she considered the trees and shrubs best suited to the city and how water could be supplied. Once Sarnia saw the beauty of Kasheron's Quarter, she was sure they would want the green and growing in their Quarters too, and then Sarnia would be a green city, not just a stone one.

Tresen's recovery continued apace and Kira sometimes wondered whether it was indeed the healing power of love. Laryia started his riding lessons and Kira happily loaned him Brightwings so they could go on short rides beyond the gate and then on longer ones as his skills and strength grew.

The days passed and Tierken had been gone over a half moon when Laryia told Kira she and Tresen were to visit Kessom. 'I need to farewell Eris, and Thalli and my other friends there,' she said. 'Would you like to come? I'm sure Tierken wouldn't mind.'

Tierken would not but Eris would, and Kira's eyes burned as she recalled her last painful conversation with the elderly Healer. She bent to remove a twig from her trousers. 'It's best you have time alone with your grandmother and your friends,' she mumbled. 'I'm happy to stay here.'

20

Once Tresen and Laryia had gone, Kira realized just how lonely the Domain could be. Queen Kiraon's garden kept her busy during the day but she had grown used to eating with Tresen and Laryia at night and chatting with them as they moved about the Domain.

She sought out Farid more often in the Meeting Hall, who was happy to share a meal and answer her questions about Terak histories, how Sarnia was administered, and anything else she asked about. Farid's initial warmth had cooled when Kira's struggle to establish the Haelen had distressed Laryia, but he had been a considerate partner at Laryia's wedding *and* afterwards, and now she discovered he also had an irreverent sense of humor.

She found herself laughing more in his company than she had in her entire time in the North and as the days slipped past and her trust in him grew, she spoke more of her life in Allogrenia, her need to make her formal farewells there, and her plans to add the green and growing to Sarnia's stone.

'It will be a fitting tribute to both brothers,' she said. 'Terak for his protection and Kasheron for his healing.'

'And to the Terak Kirillian which now include your peoples,' said Farid with a smile. 'The galloping horse *and* the allogrenia.'

Tresen and Laryia returned and the moon grew large again but there was still no sign of Tierken's patrol, and Kira's impatience turned to annoyance and then to fear. Kalos might have gone down, or the patrol come under Shargh attack, or wolf attack, or attack by some foul

Sarsalin storm. The more she thought about it, the more the possibilities of injury and death multiplied.

Farid assured her more than once that an intention to return *around the full moon* could only ever be an *intention* and that the timing of patrols was imprecise. It was just as well Healers were not *imprecise*, thought Kira irritably, as she made her way to the Illian Quarter, otherwise they would splint the legs of people with broken arms!

The Guard trailed behind her through the crisp morning air, but Kira had been to this part of the Illian Quarter often enough not to ask them for directions. She visited Atasia, wife to Borin, and distant kin to Niria, not that the kinship mattered. What did matter was Atasia was close to birthing her first child and due to a childhood accident, walked with a heavy limp.

Borin had told Kira that as a child, Atasia had gone under a wagon and been lucky to survive, but she had been unlucky too, Kira concluded acidly, to live where bone-setters were often unskilled. Atasia's limp came from a badly mended pelvis which was likely to make the birth difficult.

The door was opened after a single knock. It was Atasia's mother, Matice. 'Thank Meros you've come,' she exclaimed. 'I think it's begun.'

'But she has another moon to go,' said Kira, hurrying inside. The birth *had* started, but Kira could not take Atasia's pain. She had learned early that taking pain was only possible with injuries and illness and wondered if it were because injuries and illness *threatened* life and birthing *created* life.

The birth progressed well and Borin arrived home as the noise in the street outside began to ebb. He was an immense man, as gentle as he was big, and every time the sleeping-room door opened, she heard his rumbling voice in conversation with her Guard.

Matice came and went, her face etched with worry as she brought clean water for Kira to wash her hands, and fruited water, nuts and maizen bread for her to eat. Kira was no longer the only Tremen in Sarnia and understanding of Tremen customs, and respect for them, had spread. The night sky was full of stars before the birth neared and Kira crouched beside the bed, encouraging and instructing Atasia as she pushed, and gently turning the babe to ease it safely out. Matice cried in relief, but Atasia laughed with joy and the sound brought Borin.

Kira washed her hands and Matice produced a small package. 'I know the Tremen do not take trade for healing,' she said, 'but this is for *you*, Lady.'

Kira unwrapped the package. It was a beautifully carved mira kiraon in the spicy wood of an alwaysgreen. Niria had probably advised Matice on the gift and Kira was deeply moved by the thoughtfulness of both women. 'I thank you,' she said thickly.

She picked up her pack and paused in the doorway as she followed Matice out of the room. Borin had perched on the bed, his face full of tenderness as his immense arms cradled his wife and child, and the image stayed with Kira as she made her way up the darkened streets to the Domain and she was still thinking of Borin's love for his bondmate and child when she glanced across to the Domain stables and saw Kalos's pale shape in the yards.

Tierken was back! She sprinted across the square, leaving the Guard in her wake, and took the steps to the balcony two at a time. Her rooms were empty, as were his, and she rushed on to the Meeting Hall and flung open the door. He was in conversation with Farid, and Kira launched herself into his arms. 'You're back,' she cried in delight.

'I've been back since midday.'

'We can finish this on the morrow, if you wish, Feailner,' said Farid with a smile, already gathering the papers together, but Tierken raised his hand.

'We'll complete it now, Keeper. When I've finished here, we'll take our evening meal together, Kira,' he said, his attention on the records.

Kira smiled awkwardly and made her way from the hall. She sensed Tierken was annoyed she had not been waiting for him in the Domain, but she had waited for him *every* moment since he had gone.

He was also probably less eager for her company than she was for his, given he had doubtless spent time with his lovers. She dropped her pack onto a chair in her rooms and wearily trawled about for the owl Matice had gifted her. It had slipped to the bottom with the bracelet Tierken had traded at Mid-market and she set it on the table with the bracelet.

He had placed the bracelet on her wrist in full view of the Mid-market crowds and, according to Laryia, in doing so, had pledged to her in the Kessomi way, but not in the *Terak* way, she thought sourly. Those times seemed distant now, like the times he had looked upon her with love.

The owl had been crafted with less skill than the bracelet, but she could not help feeling it had been gifted with a more honest heart. There was a knock and she hastened to the door, hoping it was Tierken, but it was Guard Storsil. 'My Lady, Tremen Healer Arlen requests your urgent presence at the Haelen.'

Kira grabbed her pack and hurried across the Domain and down the path to the Haelen. Arlen would not summon her unless something serious had happened. He waited at the Haelen door, grim-faced. 'A burned child has been brought in, Tremen Leader. A cooking place accident, two days ago.'

'*Two days ago*?' repeated Kira in horror, as she followed Arlen between the pallets. 'Why didn't they—'

'They sought aid within the city for first. Some sort of scented lamp oil by the smell of it.'

Kira wrenched back the curtain to reveal a man and a woman embroiled in a harshly whispered argument. They fell silent but the woman's face was swollen from crying and the man looked like he had not slept for days. Kira hastened to the pallet. An oily sheen lay over the child's broken and weeping skin and only her pretty braids told Kira it was a girl.

She tried to ease the child's sleeping shirt aside but it took the skin with it, and Kira laid her hands over the material instead. The terrified child was already at the end of the tunnel, the fire licking a face unmarked and beautiful. Then Kira was back in the Haelen, fighting a fierce nausea.

The child's eyes were swollen shut but she moved her hand and the woman gasped. 'She is no longer in pain,' said Kira hoarsely. 'Speak words of love to her, reassure her, hold her.'

Kira stumbled from the alcove, grabbed a bowl, and was violently ill. She felt far worse than usual and as the room blurred, she slid down the wall, clutching the bowl in front of her. Arlen crouched beside her. 'You look most unwell, Tremen Leader.'

'I feel most unwell,' said Kira between retching.

'Will you hold down beesblest if I make some?'

'Just get me water, Arlen. When I'm feeling better, I'll go back to the Domain and sleep.'

Arlen fetched her water but that ended up in the bowl too. Then, despite Kira's protests, he lifted her onto a pallet, tucked a cover over her, and brought her a clean bowl. She needed to return to the Domain to meet with Tierken but felt too ill to get off the pallet. The cover was warm and she was weary from the long day with Atasia. She slept.

Kira sensed it was closer to morning than night when she woke. Arlen had left a lamp beside the pallet and she picked it up and made her way unsteadily to the burned child. The little girl was dead and as Kira gazed down at her, she thought of Atasia and Borin's joy at the birth of their daughter, and the grief of another mother and father at the death of theirs.

Was it Meros or Irid's will that one child should come safely into the world, while another be snatched away? she wondered, as she made her way up the Domain path. Or was it simply chance, like a spear that missed one man and impaled another. She thought of the Shargh children too who would never see their fathers again.

The sky was brilliant with stars, but she did not share Caledon's belief in their prescience or his ability to find comfort in them. They looked like shards of ice to her, cold and distant, and as unfeeling as the city's stone. What did they care for the grief of a mother or father, or for a child's suffering?

Kira stopped at the Owl Fountain, reluctant to face the emptiness of her rooms. The fountain's splash reminded her of the Drinkwater, of the water fights she'd had with

Kandor and Tresen. It was like looking back on someone else's life now; a person she scarcely recognized or knew.

'Are you going to stay there all night or come up?' It was Tierken on the balcony above.

'Come up,' she said, grateful he did not sound angry. She climbed the steps slowly, feeling nauseous again and unutterably weary. 'I beg your pardon that I didn't join you as planned,' she said when she reached him. 'I was called to the Haelen.'

'A case beyond the abilities of Healer Arlen?'

'Yes.'

'So, given that your skills are the talk of Sarnia I assume the ill person now rests comfortably.'

'No, she . . .' Nausea surged, and Kira dashed to her rooms and managed to reach the wash bowl before she vomited. She was aware of Tierken's steadying hand, but the nausea continued to wash over her in waves.

'You took her pain?' he asked, as she hung panting over the bowl.

'Yes.'

'I forbade you from doing that, not that you ever take any notice of me,' he said.

'I don't think—'

'No, you don't, do you? How ill will you become before you *do* think, about yourself *and* about those who care about you?'

Taking pain had never made her this ill before and she recalled the blisters on her forearm from Queen Kiraon's garden. She had assumed she had brushed against nettles but Niria had since told her of Northern plants that spread their poisons through the skin.

'Finished?' he asked. Kira nodded and he rinsed the bowl and moistened a cloth so she could wash her face. 'You need to sleep,' he said, taking her hand, then exclaimed and peered at her palm. 'What in Irid's name have you been doing?'

'Clearing the overgrowth from Queen Kiraon's garden. Where the alwaysgreen stump is,' she added, in response to his blank look. 'There are herbs there I need.'

'The Lady of the Domain does *not* grub about in the Wastes.' he said, as he led her to the bed. 'Sit down,' he ordered, and eased off her boots.

'Then can you trade for men to clear the growth?' said Kira, determined not to argue.

'Yes, but not this season. There's too much else to do. I'll ensure Farid arranges a supply of herbs from Kessom in the meantime. Now lie down.'

'I thank you,' she said, feeling a wave of tenderness at his concession.

'Time for sleep,' he said, and planted a kiss on her forehead.

'I want you to stay.'

'You're as white as the Silvercades, Kira. We'll breakfast together on the morrow *unless* you're called to the Haelen again.'

21

Kira still slept when Tierken returned the next morning and he paused in the doorway of the sleeping-room. His yearning for her on patrol had been so intense he had all but decided to abandon his strategy of denying her intimacy. He loathed the wariness in her face, when she looked at him, but now he was back, all the old unresolved problems crowded in again.

Once Laryia had gone, Kira would be the Lady of the Domain in every sense, and with no Marriage Walk to cement her status, it was imperative she act the part. Her unbraided hair was as wild as a young patrolman's and she still insisted on dressing like a Kessomi. Well, at least those two things could be remedied.

She turned in her sleep and as the cover slipped lower to reveal her slim shape, his want of her strengthened. He came to the bed and brought his mouth to hers and Kira's eyes jerked open and then suffused to a soft gold.

'Your time in Kessom agreed with you,' he said, as he unbuttoned her shirt and pulled it off.

She wriggled under his touch as his lips moved down her neck to her breasts. He slowed his passion to match hers, intent on feeding her need of him, and when he finally fell back, Kira perched on her elbow and turned his face to hers. 'I love you,' she said.

The declaration was painful in its intensity and his stomach clenched. *Then marry me.* The words were clear in his head, but he managed not to utter them. Since that night Marin had brought her to back to camp, he had seen her fear, anger, frustration, sadness and love, but not much happiness or contentment. That should soon change. With the Tallien gone and the Tremen leadership soon to be Tresen's, there were fewer impediments to her settling fully into life in Sarnia.

The sun was well up when he threw the cover back, aware of how much there was still to do for Laryia and Tresen's journey, but Kira's arms tightened. 'Stay, Tierken. We never have time to be together.'

'Well, I can fix that,' he said. He went to the bathing-room and ran a bath. 'If you want more time together, join me,' he called.

He smiled as Kira hesitated in the doorway. 'Haven't you shared a bath with a naked man before?'

'I have with Tresen when I was about four seasons.'

'No offence to my sister's husband, but I don't think that counts.'

Kira smiled tentatively as she took his proffered hand but when she was half in, he jerked her forward and Kira shrieked as she fell on top of him and a wave of water slopped onto the floor. 'That wasn't fair,' she spluttered.

'Ah, you don't know the rules of bathing with naked men.'

'What are they?' she demanded.

'You're about to find out,' he said mischievously.

Kira smiled as she recalled what followed, but none of it helped her with her present task of composing the message Tresen would take to Allogrenia. She remained haunted by her decision to deny the Tremen her healing and it was no comfort knowing Tresen was a skilled Healer. Whichever way she looked at it, her failure to return reeked of selfishness and sending a message, rather than going herself, made it worse. It was as if her want to be with her Terak bondmate, took precedence over the Tremen's needs.

Her churning thoughts woke the churn in her belly and she mixed a draught of silvermint and sipped it as she stared down at the blank square of paper . Tresen was right. The renunciation of the leadership must be done in person. It would be more final in her own mind too.

The understanding made writing the message simpler. She announced her bonding to the Terak Feailner and her intention to live out her days in his lands, and she undertook to return to Allogrenia before the next Turning to formally resign the leadership. In the interim, she invited the Clancouncil to take whatever action necessary to ensure the security of the Bough as the heart of Tremen healing.

It was a broad enough missive for them to elect another leader immediately, or an interim leader, or to continue as they were. The Shargh's defeat should lessen the urgency for a leader in any case and, in another season, Tierken would trust her enough to permit her travel to Allogrenia. It would be even better if they went together.

She longed to show him the pale gold of the chrysen stands, the brightwings' luminous rise at dusk, and to listen together to the cries of frostkings, hanaweys and mira kiraons as they hunted the canopy.

Kira sighed as she slipped the message into the cylinder. She would tell Tresen its contents, because he was likely to serve as interim leader or, if the Clancouncil did not want to wait, as the next leader, but she would tell no one else.

With the message done, she went to the clothing chest and retrieved one of the maps she had copied. She was keen to trace the route Tresen and Laryia would take because Tierken would likely insist she take the same route when she visited.

She knew from Tresen they were to journey south-east across the Sarsalin to Watchan Spur, the most easterly point of the Azurcades, then south-west and cross the Mahnwah River before they entered Allogrenia through the Barclan Octad.

The land between the Mahnwah and the forests was marked as Cashgar Shargh to the north, and Soushargh to the south, and Kira shivered. The route looked far longer than the route over the Azurcades, and Kira calculated the journey would take at least a moon. The eastern lands seemed emptier of groves and springs too unless she had neglected to copy them. When she had transcribed the map, she had only been interested in the way to Maraschin.

Kira still pondered the map when Tierken returned. 'Where did you get this?' he asked.

'I copied it from one in the Writing Store. I wanted to learn more about the Terak lands,' she added hurriedly. 'It seems a long way even to the edge of the forests.'

'A moon each way,' confirmed Tierken, 'but barring mishaps and foul weather, I'll be back before autumn's start.'

Kira gaped at him. '*You're* going?'

'Yes.'

'Then I can come too,' she said excitedly. It would be a pleasant journey with Tierken, Laryia and Tresen, and once they reached Allogrenia, she could renounce the leadership in person, visit the alwaysgreens where her family were buried, and make her farewells. Then she could show Tierken—

'No.'

190

'But . . . there's no reason why I can't come. I can meet with the Clancouncil and—'

His hands came to his hips. 'There are *many* reasons why you can't come, Kira. This isn't some pleasant jaunt. We must pass between the Cashgar and Soushargh lands and we both know your presence draws attacks. I won't increase the risk to Laryia because you find it hard to keep your pledge to stay here.'

'It's not about my pledge to stay here,' she said, struggling to stay calm. 'I told you I need to visit Allogrenia to properly make my farewells.'

'And we agreed you would wait.'

'But it would make sense I came, given you're to meet with the Clancouncil.'

'I never said I was to meet with the Clancouncil.'

'But if you're going to Allogrenia—'

'I never said I was going to Allogrenia either. The patrols I sent with the Lord Caledon will meet us on the northern edge of the forests and assume Laryia's protection. Then I return.'

Kira stared at him. 'But why go all the way to the Southern Forests and not visit the other part of your peoples?'

'I have the southern Rehan to rebuild and Kasheron's Quarter to make habitable,' said Tierken. 'And that's on top of the normal administrative and patrol duties of being Feailner. The journey will already cost me more time than I can afford.'

'Then don't go.'

'If my sister must journey, she will do so in safety.'

'Marin or Jonred would ensure she did so.' She paused. 'Or don't you trust their skills?'

Tierken's face hardened. 'I'm not arguing with you, Kira. You will remain here.'

Kira said nothing and he softened his voice. 'My absence will give you time to become familiar with the duties Laryia performed as Lady of the Domain but if you prefer, I will arrange an escort to take you to Kessom. Farid and Room Master Mouras can take on Laryia's duties in your absence, and we can discuss them again on my return.'

Kira kept her eyes on the table. 'I'll stay in Sarnia,' she muttered.

'Whatever you wish,' said Tierken, going to the door. None of it was what *she* wished, she thought bitterly. 'We leave before dawn. I know Laryia and Tresen will be disappointed if you're not at the stables to farewell them, as I will be, if you fail to farewell me,' he added with a smile.

'I will be there.'

The door clicked shut and Kira's gaze went to the top of the map, to Talliel, then she clenched her teeth and turned away. The two moons would pass and she would have her bondmate's Shelter again as sweet as it had been in these last nights. All she had to do was survive until then.

Caledon had been in the Southern forests less than a day with the Tremen and Terak patrols when they were abruptly surrounded by Kest and his men. There was great joy at the return of the Protector volunteers but the Terak patrolmen caused confusion and there was an uneasy stand-off.

192

Caledon ordered *all* his men to lay down their weapons but there were raucous exchanges as the Tremen volunteers yelled descriptions of the happenings beyond the forests. Kest bawled for order but it took a while for silence to fall. Caledon's return surely augured well but a swift head count revealed less than fifty of his men were Tremen and, if the rest were dead, there would be only grief at the longhouses.

'With your permission, Protector Commander, it might be quickest if I explain our presence,' said Caledon.

Kest nodded grimly and as Caledon stepped forward, the Protectors' attention swung to him. 'For those who didn't meet me on my first visit to Allogrenia, I am Caledon e Saridon e Talliel. I come now from the northern lands of your kin, the Terak *Kirillian,* to tell you that the fighting is ended and the Shargh defeated.' An immense cheer went up and Kest shut his eyes in relief.

'This is neither the place nor the time to tell of all that happened beyond Allogrenia's bounds. That is a tale of many nights and one best told by your Clanleaders, but this I can say: your leader, Feailner Kiraon of Kashclan, is safe and well in the North. The Northern Leader, the *Feailner* of the Terak *Kirillian,* who resides in the northern city of Sarnia, extends welcome to you as his kin, and invites you to visit his city and reside there if you wish.

'Some of your comrades who volunteered to fight in the North have chosen to remain in Sarnia, at least for another season. In turn, some of *their* Terak comrades, who you see here now, have come to Allogrenia.

'They do so at their Feailner's *command,* for the Feailner's sister, the Lady Laryia, has bonded with Tremen Healer Tresen. The Northern Feailner sends men to aid Allogrenia's Protectors in ensuring his sister's safety.

Healer Tresen and his bondmate, the Lady Laryia, will arrive in Allogrenia towards summer's end.'

There was an astonished silence followed by a storm of speech and while Kest's amazement matched his men's, he also noted what Caledon *had not* said. If the Northern Feailner had opened his city to the Tremen, he would expect the Tremen lands to be opened to him. Nor had Caledon mentioned when Kira would return. If she were Caledon's bondmate, Caledon would have announced it, but all he said was that she remained in the North.

Kest summoned Protector Leader Bendrash, issued him quick orders, and Bendrash led the Protectors back into the trees. 'I will journey with you, Lord Caledon,' said Kest.

Caledon nodded. 'There is much to discuss, Commander Protector, starting with the Northern Feailner's orders that once in Allogrenia, the Terak patrolmen are under your command. They are aware of their Feailner's orders,' he added.

The Terak were tall, muscular and battle-hardened and Kest was glad at the Northern Feailner's foresight. He introduced himself formally, ordered the patrol into formation and they set off with the Tremen in the lead. He and Caledon walked at the rear.

'Commander Pekrash was killed early in the fighting and Kira gave the ring of rulership to the Terak Feailner,' said Caledon, keeping his voice low. 'The Terak Feailner has commanded the Tremen since.'

Kest's breath sifted between his teeth. 'And Kira remains in the North?'

'Kira has bonded with the Terak Feailner.'

'The *Terak* Feailner,' said Kest in astonishment. 'But I thought—'

194

'That Kira would bond with me? Much happened in my absence, and in the times since, and perhaps is still to happen.'

By the time the patrols neared the Kashclan longhouse four days later, Kest knew most of what had unfolded beyond the trees including Kira's capture by the Shargh, her rescue by the Terak, and the bitter fighting since. It seemed paradoxical that while the momentous events in the North had passed them by completely, they had changed Allogrenia forever.

Even so, the Tremen had not escaped unscathed. It was hard to imagine what Kira had endured in Shargh hands but at least she had survived. Forty-eight of the Tremen volunteers had not and a host of others had been terribly injured, including Healer Tresen.

Another forty-one had delayed their return to Allogrenia, perhaps permanently, including Tremen Leader Feailner Kiraon of Kashclan, the greatest Healer Allogrenia had ever birthed.

At least Healer Tresen was to return, with a Terak bondmate, the Northern Feailner's sister no less, and forty-two *Terak* patrolmen had joined the Protectors, if temporarily. There was much the Clancouncil must deal with, the most important being the question of leadership, but they might actually set that aside, for at long last, the Bough could be rebuilt.

22

Tierken had been gone two days when Kira went back to the Wastes to work on Queen Kiraon's garden. He did not want her to *grub about* there but restoring what the first Kiraon had created was the only thing that made Sarnia bearable.

She soon understood Laryia's keenness for her friendship when she had first come to the Domain. The servers were pleasant but the *dignity* of the Domain prevented them from befriending her, or her them, and Arlen looked after the Haelen's mundane healing needs or was occupied with Resa.

That left Farid, but he was busy during the day with the building works in the Rehan and in Kasheron's Quarter, and with an endless list of administrative tasks. To speak with anyone at all during the day or share a meal with, meant seeking out Farid early before his duties began or late when they had ended.

They often breakfasted together or shared an evening meal where Farid passed on what he could of the messengers' reports from Tierken on their progress and sent back messages on the state of the building in Kasheron's Quarter and, as Kira grew to trust Farid, she shared her plans to make the stone city flower.

The moon waxed to full and then waned again, and Kira knew from Farid that Tierken's party had reached the forests. She was thankful they had arrived safely but could hardly bear to think of them in Allogrenia without her and when her frustration grew unendurable, she galloped Brightwings hard and fast down the Rehan Valley.

Brightwings was faster than the Guards' horses and while they dare not complain to her about being left behind, they had expressed their displeasure to Farid. 'The fault's not mine the Guards' horses can't keep up,' Kira had said in response to his reprimand. 'It's Tierken's,' she added. 'He gifted me the mare.'

Farid had not been amused. He had enough to do, he told her, without dealing with concerns over her safety. The Domain Guard were charged with her protection and would be punished if they failed in their duty and, if Kira were the cause of the failure, she would be responsible for their punishment.

His words revived painful memories of Slivkash's beating and Kira had stormed from the Meeting Hall, her temper not helped by knowing Farid was right and when she had calmed, she returned to apologize. Farid had hugged her, and his sympathy had brought her close to tears.

'I know it's hard for you here, Kira,' he had said. 'Why don't you go to Kessom for a time? I'm sure Eris would welcome you, as would the friends you made on your last visit.'

But Kira had shaken her head, bound by her pledge not to return.

Kashclan's celebrations at Tresen and Laryia's arrival lasted until dawn, although Tresen and Laryia had retired to their rooms well before then. The journey from Sarnia had exhausted Tresen, as had comforting Laryia in their travel through the trees. Given how cheerful she had been on their journey south, Tresen had been shocked by her distress in having to farewell Tierken.

She had clung sobbing to her grim-faced brother while Tresen had stood uncomfortably by. She had tearfully assured Tresen of her love many times since but it had not lessened his guilt in taking her from her home or his anxiety for Kira, whose face had been filled with despair as they had ridden away.

Caledon had been accommodated at the Kashclan longhouse, which suited him, as he wanted to spend time with Miken. The Kashclan leader served as the unofficial Tremen Leader but that was not the only reason Caledon sought his company. It was men like Miken and Kemrick of Tarclan, and the Morclan leader Marren, who were key to the survival of the fragile Terak-Tremen reunification and Caledon's increasingly urgent star-thoughts insisted the reunification *must* survive.

The Northern triumph over the Shargh had as much potential to seed war as it had to seed peace. Tierken had fought with the ruthlessness true of the Terak line, an inclination for brutality kept dormant by a long peace that had disguised the loss of the Terak's healing part. Now made strong by victory and their hatred of the Shargh renewed, it would take little provocation for the Terak to scour the Shargh settlements from the lands, and even turn their swords on the Ashmiri.

Nowhere in the stars was the murder of innocents condoned, even given that the child who ran singing through the trees, could one day grow to be the warrior who killed and there were certainly none among the Tremen, the Terak's healing part, who would permit such slaughter. But the Tremen themselves were vulnerable, as events had shown.

The breach between Kasheron and Terak, that had left both peoples like broken-winged birds, had been mended by the coming together of Kira and Tierken, and that hard-won wholeness must not be allowed to fracture anew.

Caledon wondered too, as he sat in speech with Miken, whether the stars' want for wholeness was so great that they had brought Tresen and Laryia together as well, to ensure their purposes were fulfilled. The joining of the Terak Feailner's only sister with the man who must surely become the Tremen Leader was more than chance, but Caledon did not yet know whether Tresen and Laryia's marriage was intended to strengthen the unifying effect of Kira and Tierken's bonding, or *replace it* should it break.

'My bond-daughter seems to be settling well,' said Miken. 'Tenerini and I are already fond of her.'

Caledon nodded. 'The Lady Laryia is well loved in the North.'

'Do you journey to your home in Talliel when you leave us, or visit the Tain King?' asked Miken.

'Talliel, most probably,' said Caledon. He missed his sister and her daughters, especially Pisa, and knew his father fretted for him, but Caledon also knew his decision must wait until he cleared the trees and saw what the stars told. Only then would he know which way to turn his feet. Tarkenda ducked into the top scrcha, drew a bowl of sherat and gulped it down. 'Orsron's dead,' she said.

'What?' gasped Palansa, hoping she had misheard.

Tarkenda drew a second bowl. 'Orsron, Sansula's son. He sickened during the night, burned like fire coals, and now he's dead.' She clicked her fingers. 'Just like that.'

Palansa brought a shaking hand to her mouth. 'Poor Sansula,' she choked, but her thoughts darted to three days before, when they had sat together in the reed beds and played with their sons. She hurried to the sling and laid her hand on Ersalan's forehead. He was no warmer than usual, but her heart continued its frantic beat.

'Arkendrin's gone too,' said Tarkenda.

'What, dead?' asked Palansa, grappling with this next piece of astonishing news.

'No, gone, left,' said Tarkenda, and lowered herself onto a stool. 'He's taken Irdodun and Irdodun's lesser blood-ties and gone.'

'But where? Why?'

'For the gold-eyed Healer,' said Tarkenda sourly. 'What else but the Healer's death can restore the vision to his rotting eye? Cure his lameness? Grant him your son's death, your body, and the highest Sorcha on the Grounds? What else but the *creature's* destruction stands between him and all he so richly deserves?'

Palansa sat heavily and searched Tarkenda's face. 'Have you *seen* this?' Tarkenda did not answer and Palansa caught her hand. 'Have you?'

'I've told you what I've seen! The Healer will be here and there will be death but *seeing* isn't enough. We already have an abundance of death and her death won't stop ours.'

'But the Telling suggests *our* suffering will end,' countered Palansa. '*Deeds long past will hunt the Shargh and funeral smoke consume the stars until the thing that draws no breath, devours the dark that feeds on death,*' she recited.

'It *would* end if we were all dead,' pointed out Tarkenda. 'You forget the Healer breathes even as we do. Whatever the *thing* is, it's not her.' A wailing sounded down the slope and Palansa blanched. 'It might not be

Sansula's blood-ties,' cautioned Tarkenda. 'Warriors still die from the fighting or from the water in their lungs.'

'Maybe they brought back the evil that killed Orsron,' said Palansa fearfully. 'Maybe the thing that *draws no breath* is some vile pestilence the Northerners seeded. Maybe they won't need to come here to destroy us!' she all but shrieked.

Tarkenda seized her by the shoulders. 'Calm yourself,' she ordered.

'I'm frightened for Ersalan,' whispered Palansa.

'Sometimes babes die,' said Tarkenda, although it was unusual for them to die so quickly, or so unexpectedly. Orsron had been a lusty little boy, not like some babes who were born sickly and succumbed to even the smallest ill. But voicing her fears would not help Palansa stay strong, and Palansa *must* be strong for what was to come.

'Keep Ersalan within until we see how things unfold,' she said. 'Orsron might have taken a chill or been born with some flaw only the Sky Chiefs knew of, and with Arkendrin gone, there's one less risk to Ersalan.'

Palansa's anxious expression did not ease. 'For a now,' she said.

Six days after autumn's start *and* after Tierken should have returned, Kira thrust nuts and fruit into her pack and set off on Brightwings down the Rehar. She wanted a long ride to exhaust her enough to sleep and when she finally reached the valley's mouth, she let Brightwings have her head.

The mare stretched out in a hard gallop and Kira stood in the stirrups and laughed as the wind rushed through her hair. The mare's speed eased her frustration but when she finally glanced over her shoulder, it was to a plain empty of Guard. They were probably just beyond the last rise, or the one before that and she checked Brightwings, intending to circle back, when she saw movement ahead. She glanced over her shoulder again, anxiously this time, but whoever approached was unlikely to be Shargh.

She shaded her eyes and the movement finally resolved itself into silver horses. Tierken's patrol at last! She urged Brightwings back to a gallop and did not slow until she reached him. 'Welcome home, my Lord,' she said smiling, and then bowed as his men did, but there was no answering smile.

Farid's messages told Tierken of Kira working in the Wastes, despite her undertaking not to, while the *messengers* told of Sarnia's gossip, of the *Feailner's woman* laughing with the Keeper, both late at night and early in the morning, the inference clear that she enjoyed his company in between as well.

The gossip undermined Kira's already tenuous position and now she greeted him with all the impudent freedom of a Caru woman, loose on the plain, the Guard who accompanied a *Lady of the Domain*, nowhere to be seen.

'Where are your Guard?' he demanded.

'Just a little behind. I wanted to give Brightwings—'

'So far behind they can't be seen! My orders were that you *not* go *anywhere* without them!'

Tierken's position as Feailner, and the silence of his watching men, demanded Kira bow her head and beg his pardon, but her fury built instead. She had spent two long moons longing for his return, and he had not even the grace to smile at her, let alone greet her.

'You confuse me with your men, *my Lord*,' she said, using the title ironically now. 'I'm not a patrolman and I'm not yours to command.' And with that, she wrenched Brightwings around and galloped back towards Sarnia, passing the disconcerted Guard and only slowing when it was too dark to see. The Guard still had not caught up by the time she reached the Domain stables and by then her anger had given way to shame.

A Terak Feailner must always be that in front of his men, Caledon had warned her. Kira hurried up the balcony steps to her rooms, nauseous again due to her upset, and wanting only to crawl into bed. Instead she bathed, using the soap Tierken liked, and brushed out her hair in front of the fire. She would beg his pardon when he came later and pledge never to defy him in public again.

The patrol should not be too far behind, she thought as she settled at the table, but the fire burned low and the next thing she knew Niria was setting down her breakfast. 'You should take your rest in your bed, Lady,' she chided.

'Is the Feailner breakfasting in the Meeting Hall?' asked Kira, rubbing her stiff neck.

'I believe he and the Keeper are inspecting building works,' said Niria, as she poured Kira cotzee. 'Is there something else I can get for you, Lady?'

'No . . . I thank you.' Niria bustled out but Kira stayed where she was. She understood why Tierken was angry, but he had shunned her after almost two moons apart, two moons when she had thought of him every day, *longed* for him every day. It might not prove he had other lovers elsewhere but it proved he had no love for her.

Tierken finished going through the trading records with Farid and then they sat together over the remains of their breakfast, drinking mugs cotzee. The rebuilding of the southern Rehan had been completed in his absence and the houses in Kasheron's Quarter progressed well. All was in order and further advanced than he had dared hope possible. His relationship with the trader leaders had strengthened too, in fact, his feailnership would be at its most settled and successful, if it were not for the antics of *his woman*.

'I take a patrol north at the new moon,' he said.

Farid looked at him in surprise. 'So soon?'

'It's nearly nine moons since I've patrolled that way and its time the herders in the southern Ashkal are reacquainted with their Feailner.'

'I meant you won't have been back long. Kira misses you terribly.'

'I'll be instructing Kira on her responsibilities in the Domain before I go. She will have more than enough to occupy herself in my absence. You and Room Master Mouras have too much to do without taking on her duties as well. And I'll be speaking to Kira of other matters, one of which I must raise with you now.' Farid glanced at his face and set down his mug.

'We both know how the gossip runs in Sarnia and that the loose tongues would have had you and Laryia married a dozen times, but Laryia's reputation remained intact because she knew how to conduct herself. Kira doesn't. Thus far I've been patient, but there's a limit to what I can tolerate when talk on the street says she shares your bed.'

Farid stared at him in shock. 'Tierken—'

'No doubt there are reasons why she takes her last meal of the day *and* her first with you but along with her refusal to marry, her inappropriate dress, her working like a hand-trader in the Wastes, and her going where she pleases without the Domain Guard, it is enough to make her position in the Domain untenable.

'I hardly need to remind you that such innuendo undermines the authority you *must* have to administer Sarnia effectively while I patrol. Given that, I request you don't spend time alone with Kira. If you must speak with her, ensure a server is present or speak to her in the square or in another public place.'

'Tierken, I—'

'I've asked Niria to send Kira here at midday and will speak to her of this and other matters. Is there anything else we need to discuss, Keeper?'

Farid swallowed dryly. 'No, Feailner.'

'Then we'll meet on the morrow to go over the provisioning of the next patrol.'

23

Tierken still did not greet Kira when she entered the Meeting Hall, just motioned her to a seat and started outlining the duties that Laryia had performed as *Lady of the Domain*. Even when Kira interrupted him to beg his pardon for her behavior on the plain, his demeanor did not change. Nor did he acknowledge her apology. His indifference confirmed Kira's conclusion his love for her was no more and she struggled to focus on his words.

'It is important you are clear on your responsibilities in the Domain before I leave on my next patrol,' he was saying.

'Your *next* patrol?' Her heart thudded sickeningly in her throat. He obviously had a lover he was keen to return to. 'You've only just returned from the last patrol and that was more than two moons!'

'That was an *escort* not a patrol. Despite *not* being Terak, I thought you understood a Terak Feailner ensured the security of *all* Terak lands and people, not just those enclosed by Sarnia's wall.'

'And what am I supposed to do in your absence?'

'That's what I am outlining now,' said Tierken impatiently. 'Apart from maintaining the smooth running of the Domain, you can spend time repairing the damage you've done to your reputation.'

'Damage?'

'I'm not a herder, Kira, nor a woodcutter, nor a patrolman. If I were, it wouldn't matter to Sarnia if you dressed in trousers and wandered about alone, if you married or refused to, if you took lovers—'

'If *I* took lovers?' gasped Kira, gripping the table to steady herself.

'You're naive if you think joining Farid in the Meeting Hall last thing at night, and emerging first thing in the morning, won't fuel gossip that you share his bed.'

'*You* think Farid and I are lovers?' she choked out.

'It's what Sarnia thinks that matters! I've spoken to Farid and he understands the need to protect your reputation as well as his own. You've been in Sarnia over eight moons, Kira. It's time you became—'

'Terak? I told you early in our time together I would always be Tremen,' she said bitterly. 'I was honest about that.'

'I've arranged for Mouras to meet with you here later this day,' continued Tierken, as if she had not spoken. 'I need to inspect the building works in Kasheron's Quarter now.'

'I'm to meet the Room Master alone? Aren't you afraid I'll take him as a lover?'

Tierken paused at the door. 'If there's anything in Mouras's instructions you don't understand, you can ask me on my return,' he said, and the door clicked shut behind him.

Mouras was kindly but he spoke exceptionally slowly and as soon as she was able, Kira muttered an excuse about feeling unwell and returned to her rooms. It was not entirely untrue; she did feel queasy again, probably due to her churning thoughts.

She took to her bed early, feeling weary and knowing that Tierken would not come, and woke the next morning to the sounds of Niria building the fire in the next room.

Kira knew she should rise, bathe and change, but she curled into a ball and analysed her exchange with Tierken the previous day.

There was still curiosity about her in Sarnia, but apart from the time Rosham had spat at her, she had heard no sly whisperings or muttered insults. And she certainly had not noticed anything that suggested Sarnia thought her unfaithful to Tierken. It was the same when she healed in the Haelen. Those who sought aid were genuinely respectful and their gifts showed a sensitive acceptance of her Tremen ways.

Niria hovered in the doorway and she roused. 'I'm sorry to disturb you, Lady, but the Feailner asked that you breakfast with him in the Meeting Hall, and that was a little time ago now. I've laid out the gowns the Lady Laryia traded for you.'

Kira leapt out of bed, not wanting another quarrel with Tierken by being late, and barely paused to smooth down her clothing before she hurried along the balcony. Farid was in the Meeting Hall too and she returned his smile as she joined them at the table.

'Did Niria neglect to bring you the gowns?' asked Tierken, his gaze on her crumpled shirt.

'No, she—'

'Then why are you wearing Kessomi garb?'

'It's Tremen,' said Kira, and braced wearily for another fight.

'We'll wait for you while you change,' said Tierken.

Kira glanced from Farid's sympathetic face to Tierken's hard one and some part of her knew they had reached an ending, as inevitable as the death of early shoots under late snow. 'I don't intend to change, Tierken,' she said. 'As I've told you before, I'm Tremen, not Terak.'

Farid moved uncomfortably in his chair and Tierken's jaw clenched. 'No response to that, Feailner?' she goaded, unable to keep the bitterness from her voice. 'But then again, I can understand why you don't want the unpleasantness of an argument inflicted on Farid, on your *best* friend, *who you don't trust with me!*'

There was a blur as Tierken seized her arm and half wrenched her over the table. His other hand swung back and Farid gave a warning cry, but all Kira saw was the flash of the ring that Tierken wore. *You will obey me in the end, Kiraon,* her father had said, after the blow, but there was no blow. Tierken released her and Kira staggered backwards.

Farid was on his feet, but Kira kept her gaze on Tierken. There was a long silence and then she bowed low because that was what you did when you left a Feailner, went steadily to the door, and closed it quietly behind her. The same calmness stayed with her as she made her way along the balcony to her rooms, filled her pack with every bit of food she could find, thrust her sword down the side, and folded the map on top. The calmness even endured as she went to the stables, saddled Brightwings, and clipped a full waterskin to the harness.

'Where would you ride, Lady?' asked Storsil.

'Just to the end of the Rehan. There's no need to bring food or water.'

Birds rose from the Rehan River and when she reached the houses, people bowed, and Kira waved but it were as if someone else sat astride the mare, watched the shadows lengthen, listened to the hoofbeats of the following Guard.

When she reached the valley's mouth, she stopped and turned to them. 'I thank you for your care of me during my time in the North,' she said, then dug her heels into

Brightwings' side. The mare leapt away, and Kira urged her to greater and greater speed.

The Guard would follow through the night and the next day, but in the end, a lack of food and water would force them back to Sarnia. Two days out and two days back gave her a four-day start on pursuers. She clenched her teeth, crouched lower, and thundered on.

End of The Kira Chronicles series: Book 5 The Crying of Birds

Discover the ending of Kira's story in Book 6 The Music of Home or enjoy the whole series in a single book: The Kira Chronicles – Complete 6 Book Series

Take a peek at Book 6

It was close to midday when Kira became aware of a grey cloud to the west. She stared at it as she rode, reminded of the snow clouds that had forced the patrol to Ember Keep on her first journey north. She was not far from the same spot, she realized uneasily.

Tierken had said that if you were going to get early snow, it would be between Cover-cape Crest and the Breshlin. Her mouth twisted. Despite her best intentions, the Northern Feailner had slipped into her thoughts, but he was the least of her worries.

Kira hoped the cloud would simply go away, but it rolled inexorably closer until it extinguished the sun. It was not a cloud, she realized as it enclosed her in a clammy blanket, it was fog.

Within a dozen paces she could scarcely see a length in front, and a half- dozen paces later, she had no idea where south was. It would be pointless riding in circles, or even worse, riding north again and she dismounted and let Brightwings graze. The mare tore at the grass contentedly but as Kira's weariness grew, she knotted her hands in Brightwings' mane and dozed against her for warmth and comfort. The fog darkened and it was deep in the night when the mare's head suddenly shot up. The fog was impenetrable and after a while Brightwings resumed her grazing. Kira remained rigid. There might be Guard nearby but there might also be Shargh.

At least it would be dawn soon, hopefully the fog gone, and she on her way to the alwaysgreens' shelter at Cover-cape Crest. 'You'll like the grove,' she murmured to Brightwings. 'It's—' The mare snorted, wild-eyed as a dark shape launched itself at Kira. She was knocked off her feet and as her head thumped the ground, a disfigured face thrust close, its lips drawn back in a macabre smile, as rough hands fastened around her throat.

I hope you enjoyed *The Crying of the Birds Book 5 in The Kira Chronicles Series.* **Authors need reviews!** It is how our readers find us. I would love you to leave me an honest review on Amazon, Goodreads, or another of your favourite reader sites. Read on to discover my other books.

Works by K S Nikakis
Available on Amazon KDP and a range of digital platforms.

Non Fiction

Journey: Seeking the Sacred, Spirit and Soul in the Australian Wilderness

When we set out into the wilderness, what is it we really seek?

Do we seek new sights or do we seek new selves? And are we really on one journey or on two?

Journeying fifteen thousand kilometres into Australia's blood-red heart, Nikakis discovers that every journey is perilous, for travellers risk carrying the clutter of their outer lives with them; a clutter that blinds them to the other journey they crave; that of the inner soul-journey into a deeper understanding of self.

To enter Australia's vast Outback wilderness, is to enter a place of endless horizons; a place doused with brilliant gold dawns and dazzling sunsets; a place silvered by star-encrusted night skies and, most importantly, a place of hidden sacred places in whose deep stillness our inner journeys can at last unfold.

In the spirit of travellers like Robert Macfarlane and Scott Stillman, Nikakis asks what it is we really see, feel and understand when we follow in the steps of those who have gone before us deep into the wilderness.

Drawing on her Ph.D. in Joseph Campbell's hero myth, and using original poetry and novel extracts, Nikakis takes us on this second journey; a journey of the sacred, spirit and soul, where our inner selves finally have the time and space to gift us richer and more fully-realised lives.

Fantasy Novel Series

Angel Caste 5 Book Series – available complete in one book or as five individual books: Angel Blood, Angel Breath, Angel Bone, Angel Bound, Angel Blessed.

Angel Caste – Complete 5 Book Series - *a modern female hero on a timeless quest*

A troubled half-angel, a beautiful angel guide, a binding promise . . .

Viv is on day release from jail to attend the funeral of the thug she thinks is her father, when she comes face to face with her real father, the powerful angel Archae Kald. If finding out she's a half-angel isn't shocking enough, Viv discovers her mother isn't dead after all but lost somewhere in the tangle of worlds called the Rynth.

Determined to find the only person who has ever truly loved her, Viv goes to Kald's angel world where he appoints the beautiful Thris as her guide. Thris is kind and caring, unlike the males Viv has known before, but after living on the streets, Viv finds it almost impossible to trust.

Friendship grows as Thris trains her to travel the rifts, but the Rynth is a dark and dangerous place, even for angels and, as Thris grows increasingly tempted by Viv's emerging angel traits, disaster strikes.

Viv journeys on alone and stumbles into a war zone where she finds a lost child. She pledges to take the child to safety but, as the war rages on, deciding who is friend and who is enemy becomes a deadly game of chance.

Bound by his promise to guide Viv to her mother, Thris embarks on a desperate search for her, but a greater threat confronts them both and, in the end, they must fight not just for their own lives, but for the lives of those they love.

The Kira Chronicles - 6 Book Series – available complete in one book or as six individual books: The Whisper of Leaves, The Silence of Stone, The Secrets of Stars, The Thunder of Hoofs, The Crying of Birds, The Music of Home.

The Kira Chronicles – Complete 6 Book Series – *traditional fantasy with deep forests and high stakes*

A gold-eyed Healer, a prophecy, two brothers at war.

In seasons long past, twin gold-eyed princes sundered a kingdom. Rejecting his brother Terak's warrior ways, Kasheron led his people deep into the great southern forests and established the healing settlement of Allogrenia. The Tremen flourished, upholding Kasheron's legacy of peace and healing, and protected by the vast, trackless trees.

All Tremen delight in the healing arts, but Kira is the greatest Healer of them all.

To the north of Allogrenia, drought ravages the Shargh's land, and as their suffering escalates, the chief's younger brother seizes on an ancient prophecy to snatch the chiefship for himself. The prophecy links the Shargh's doom to a gold-eyed Healer, and Kira has gold eyes.

The Shargh attack with devastating consequences and Kira must fight to save the wounded, but the Shargh wounds rot, no matter her skill, and Kira finds herself in a deadly race against time. As the slaughter continues, she makes the horrifying discovery that the Shargh hunt her. To halt the attacks and save her people, she sets off for the North to seek aid from her long sundered warrior kin.

But the dangers beyond the forests exceed even the Shargh attacks. The Tremen detest their warrior kin but Terak's descendants have inflicted a worse fate on the Tremen. Kira's new-found love is torn apart by ancient hostilities and when trust turns to betrayal, it risks everything she fought for.

As the battles rage on, Kira becomes increasingly sickened by the bloodshed. Desperate to end the suffering once and for all, she sets out on a quest that could cost her everything and everyone she loves.

Fantasy Novels

The Emerald Serpent – *the Celtic Fae in a fight for survival*

Book trailer: https://www.youtube.com/watch?v=bGpKxnpCEMg

Betrayal, torture, death: Etaine lives on only to destroy those who robbed her of everything she loved.

Seven years before, Etaine met fellow Ranger Cormac, the he-Eadar she believed was her longed-for true-mate. Emerald-eyed, white-skinned, and black-haired, the Eadar had formed into Ranger bands to fight the Fada, invading religious zealots determined to replace the Eadar's Serpent Goddess with their own gods of stone.

The pure blood of the ancient Eadar runs strong in Etaine and Cormac's veins, and their joining had the potential to open the Emerald and Serpent Ways to them, old worlds only true Eadar can enter. But their love affair goes tragically amiss, with catastrophic consequences.

Etaine flees and as the years pass, slowly rebuilds her life, but the Fada's attacks grow more ferocious, and the Eadar are forced to fight for their very existence. When the Fada mass to commit yet more bloody slaughter, and the bands join in a final, desperate effort to defeat them, Etaine comes under Cormac's command, the very last Eadar she ever wants to see again.

Together they have a weapon that can destroy the Fada, but to use it, Etaine must learn to trust again and Cormac to Remember. And time runs short: the Serpent rises.

Heart Hunter – *a female hunter on an impossible quest*

Fleet is a young Sceadu hunter: skilled, strong, and fast. She hunts deep into the icy mountains, seeking meat for her people, for the rains have failed and plunged the Sceaudu into hunger.

Her hunts are hard, but she has much to look forward to. Soon she will be gifted her air-name by the Sceadu's shaman, and then she will be a full adult, and free to marry the man she loves.

But while Fleet is on hunt, the old shaman dies, and the new shaman visions a very different future for her: cross the frozen, ice-locked mountains and complete a perilous quest or lose the man she loves forever.

In a moment of anger and frustration, Fleet commits a terrible wrong and sets out into the frigid mountains to atone with her life. In a journey that takes her deep into the earth's darkest places, into strange new worlds, and even into Death itself, she discovers that only she can save her people. To survive, she must draw on every shred of her hunter strength, and doing the impossible, it turns out, is just the beginning.

The Third Moon – *science fantasy with a very human quest*

Where does the past end and the future begin?

Haunted by inherited memories of his people's dispossession and theft of their children, Warrain is just twelve years old when the nightmare repeats. But Warrain isn't living on Earth in the 21st Century, he is living on the planet Imago in the far flung future.

Five years before, Station One's Mech's got high on the opioid arrash, and in the bloodshed that followed, Warrain's scientific community were expelled from the Station, his father murdered, and his mother and unborn sibling lost to him.

The scientists carve out a rudimentary Station high in Imago's ranges, and Warrain's friends get on with their lives. Not Warrain; he climbs the Tors to stare down at Station One, dream of his mother and sibling, and plot revenge.

And then one day, everything changes. A third moon appears in the sky, one of Imago's life-forms calls him by name, and disease breaks out at Station One.

When the Mechs visit to seek help for their ill, Warrain seizes the opportunity to deal them a blow they will never forget. But the third moon brings changes that threaten them all and, to aid the life-form whose kind is being dispossessed and slaughtered, he must turn his back on the hate that has long sustained him and find another way to live.

Messenger – *a dystopic future filled with hope*

In a world made deaf by hatred, who will hear the messenger?

Severine's world ends the day her family is murdered. Being raised in the loving community of gay Travelers always marked her as an outsider, but being female puts her in mortal danger. Women are scarce, precious, and hunted.

When chance brings Severine face to face with the father she has never known, he assigns the son of his murdered best friend to guard her. They soon clash. Severine believes all men are violent brutes and Jeph resents his freedoms being curtailed.

An uneasy understanding grows but Jeph is glad to deliver her to the Enclaves, a sanctuary her father has carved out in the mountains for his women and children. But there is no safety in a world broken by war and sickness and when violence follows her, Severine flees to the northern city of Andhaka in search of a home amongst her mother's people. Jeph follows, bound by loyalty to her father, but the north holds terrible dangers for him.

It's been years since Andhaka has welcomed outsiders with anything but bullets, and to survive and to protect Jeph, Severine must learn to use her enemies' weapons against them. As the stakes rise, she comes to understand the horror of her mother's loss, and what drove her father north seventeen years before. His quest becomes her quest, but she hasn't counted on the savage legacy that war and sickness have left behind, or on falling in love.

I Heard the Wolf Call My Name – *gender-fluid shifters in search of home*

Finalist Best YA Novel, Aurealis Awards, 2019

Jax is just twelve years old and in bird-form high above his island home, when it explodes, killing everyone on it. He believes he is the only survivor until ten years later, he comes face to face with his boyhood friend, Matiu.

Matiu is military and the military need shifters for a crucial mission, but Jax refuses. Having spent ten long years burying his bizarre shifter past, he isn't about to resurrect it. But Matiu rouses other feelings too that Jax finds harder to ignore.

As the military ramps up pressure to force Jax's cooperation, he shifts to bird-form and flees to the last remaining island where he crash lands in the middle of Anahera's vision-quest. She searches for her skin-spirit animal to transform her into a protector of her people, and dreams of finding the white-wolf, but finds Jax instead. To save him she must abandon her quest but her kindness only adds to Jax's turmoil.

To decide who he truly is and where he really belongs, he must first confront his painful past, but that isn't the worst of his problems. The forces that blew Jax's island out of existence now threaten Anahera's as well, and he might just be the only shifter who can save it.

And time is running out.

Fantasy Short Stories

The Gift – A Deep Fantasy Short Story #1 – free on my website at www.ksnikakis.com

Excerpt:

Thariel sat for a long time, surveying all around her, as if she ate the world that would soon be memory. Then she took the harness from the mare, and with soft words, thanked her and bade her farewell. Her own feet she turned towards the forest, tossing her face-plate aside as she went, so that her hair fell loose to her waist, then she discarded her chest-armour, the sword and dagger, her bow and quiver.

The trees closed in and she came at last to the lake Men call Menios and stood for a while on its shore. An owl cried and a mouse shrieked, and all around her the souls of the newly dead jostled in their journey to the void. She stepped into the water and the new life inside her quivered.

'Fear not, little one,' she whispered, in her own tongue. 'We are going home.'

The Tale of Prince Anura – A Deep Fantasy Short Story

#2 – free on my website at www.ksnikakis.com

Excerpt:

I should have been happy, for she was beautiful. Dark rivers of curls, skin as white as moonlight on water, breasts softer than spawn, and she loved me well. But her chamber was small, no matter the comfort of her bed, and the old feelings of entrapment rose, as persistent as gas that bubbles from rot below still waters.

I sat at the casement and listened, as I had once loitered near the watery skin of the second world and waited. The moon grew large and small many times, but it came at last, as I knew it would. The soft lament on the night-time air, the song of a soul as confined as mine. It took me a journey of many days through the depths of a massive forest to find her tower.

Stone it was and sheer, and as remote as the third world's glimmer had once been. I sang to her and she answered with sweet melodies of her own and we made love as frogs do, with our voices. And when trust had built, she let down her shining ladder of golden hair.

Glass-Heart – A Deep Fantasy Short Story #3

Finalist Best YA Short Story, Aurealis Awards, 2019

Excerpt:

Geth moved amongst his band, exchanging quiet words while they waited. Some he had fought with since the Tallon's foul ships had first found their shores while others had come later, when the burn of cot and kin had sent them from their valleys.

Hate drove them but hate was no shield against arrow and knife. It was fighting skills that kept them hale, and Geth ensured they had them aplenty. He needed them living, not just for their own sakes and his, but for what would come later. When the Tallon's stain had been scoured away, the destroyed must be rebuilt.

Kyth sat alone and he went to her and gazed about. 'The glass-heart's fled, has it?'

'I sent her to a place of safety. She will come to me when it is over.'

'Safety was what I wanted for you!'

'And what I wanted for Nyar.' Her eyes caught the star-sheen as she looked up at him. 'But you can't always have what you want, can you, Ceannasai?'

Dragon Sprite – A Deep Fantasy Short Story #4

Excerpt:

Genn rocketed straight upwards, not just because she enjoyed seeing the limitless blue sky before her, but because a Waiwin's wing shape made vertical flight harder for them. Orin didn't try to catch her but swept in circles around her, gaining height in an ever-narrowing spiral. It was a clever tactic and one Genn didn't believe he had thought of in the instant she had cleared the trees. He had obviously studied her strategies and developed a plan to counter them or so he thought.

Genn waited until the spiral narrowed to axeel, the minimum distance a Waiwin must keep from a Velven unless she accepted him, then swerved towards him, narrowing the distance between them. Orin's eyes flashed to black, shocked she had accepted him, but before he could act, she folded her wings and dropped.

The strength that had driven Orin's pursuit had surged to his wing-tendrils in anticipation of locking them with hers and he would struggle even to stay airborne until it flowed back.